Normal for Norfolk

(The Thelonious T. Bear Chronicles)

Mitzi Szereto

Co-authored with Teddy Tedaloo

Thelonious T. Bear Books

Praise for
Normal for Norfolk (The Thelonious T. Bear Chronicles)

"For anyone who's ever wondered what *Paddington at Large* would have been like if it had been written by Raymond Chandler—and who hasn't?—Mitzi Szereto has the answer. Like Philip Marlowe, Szereto's Thelonious T. Bear is a modern knight errant who plays it cool even as the light of suspicion shines on him. And like Paddington, he's short of stature and long on charm. If you like your sleuths tough, cynical and cute as a button, *Normal for Norfolk* is the book for you."

—**Steve Hockensmith**, author of *Holmes on the Range* and *Pride and Prejudice and Zombies: Dawn of the Dreadfuls*

"A rural crime novel I found approachable and engaging, featuring an oddly detached hero who just happens to be a small bear.... I enjoyed my visit to Norfolk and I could certainly *bear* another outing (sorry)!"
— ***The American* magazine**

"*Normal for Norfolk* has it all: magic, gritty realism, humor, cultural commentary, intelligence, charm, and suspense. The hero of this novel, Thelonious T. Bear, finds himself at the heart of a mystery. He's a photojournalist like no other, a pub-loving, anthropomorphized bear who wears cologne and a deerstalker hat. I am eager to read the next book in Mitzi Szereto's series."
—**Janice Eidus**, author of *The War of the Rosens* and *The Last Jewish Virgin*

Normal for Norfolk (The Thelonious T. Bear Chronicles)
Copyright © 2012 by Mitzi Szereto (co-authored with Teddy Tedaloo)

All rights reserved.
Except for brief passages quoted in newspaper, magazine, radio, television, or online reviews, no part of this book may be reproduced in any form or by any means, electronic or mechanical, including photocopying or recording, or by information storage or retrieval system, without permission in writing from the author. Please do not participate in or encourage electronic piracy of copyrighted materials in violation of the author's rights. Purchase only authorized editions.

Published by Thelonious T. Bear Books
Thelonious T. Bear Books is an imprint of Midnight Rain Publishing.
www.midnightrainpublishing.com

www.mitziszereto.com
www.teddytedaloo.com

Cover design: Caramelo Moon
Cover photo: Mitzi Szereto

Publication Data is on file at U.S. Copyright Office, Library of Congress, United States of America.

This book is a work of fiction. Names, characters, places and incidents are the product of the author's imagination or are used fictitiously. Any resemblance to actual persons, living or dead, events, locales or businesses is entirely coincidental.

Normal for Norfolk (often abbreviated as NFN or N4N) is an expression used in certain parts of England to denote something that is weird or peculiar. The term is believed to have originated with doctors in the county of Norfolk as a form of medical shorthand to categorise patients whom they considered to have peculiar habits or who were "intellectually challenged." These kinds of individuals were thought to be so common to the region that they were deemed normal as far as Norfolk was concerned. Although considered derogatory because of its portrayal of those from the county as strange or peculiar, the expression has been embraced by the people of Norfolk as a term of endearment as well as an indication of their ability to laugh at themselves.

Prologue

Popular Village Publican Found Bludgeoned to Death!
—Front page headline from the *Walsham Courier*

THELONIOUS T. BEAR REACHED UP to adjust his deerstalker hat against the Norfolk wind. It was kicking up something fierce, and he didn't fancy losing his most favoured of fashion accessories, particularly when he'd only just bought the thing. He'd had a devil of a time finding one that fit properly, returning several before finally hitting on the right one—and he wasn't about to go through that whole rigmarole again. Buying online had its advantages, but it also had its disadvantages. Each visit to the post office with yet another rewrapped parcel caused Thelonious's gut to churn. Buying clothing and accessories online was all well and good, providing the item you ordered actually *fit*. When it didn't, well…it was no wonder he'd ended up being burdened with so many unusable items, preferring to be out a few quid rather than endure the stares and sniggers of postal employees. The ones who worked at his local branch were particularly unpleasant, especially that Asian woman with the loud voice who always shouted at him as if he were hard of hearing. Thelonious's hearing was perfectly fine, thank you very much, but it wouldn't be fine for much longer if he had to keep visiting the post office. Maybe this Mrs. Singh or whatever her name was should see her GP about being fitted for a deaf aid. If Thelonious had to work alongside her, he'd be filing a complaint about his work conditions with the employment tribunal!

Standing at the edge of the road alongside his Mini Cooper with the Union Jack painted on the roof, Thelonious stretched the kinks out of his neck and shoulders and stared up at the endless expanse of afternoon sky. It was as if he'd suddenly found himself perched at the edge of the world; the streaky ceiling of blue above was so close he could've reached up to touch it. The salt tang of the North Sea teased his nostrils and he breathed deeply, smelling fish and various creatures that lived on the bottom of the sea. Thelonious was hungry; starving, in fact. He'd been driving since morning, a journey that had been made longer due to the intrusive presence of speed cameras on the A roads and the narrow winding B roads, not to mention having to pull over several times to peruse his road atlas when the car's SATNAV became confused and kept sending him round in circles. Frankly, Thelonious was confused himself. That was the thing about the countryside—it all looked the same after a while; he was certain he'd been travelling the same bit of road more than once. No matter, he wasn't in any hurry. He'd finally arrived in Norfolk, where he planned to spend the next few weeks, if not months—just him and his trusty camera and the wide-open unpolluted Norfolk skies.

Unlike many in his field, Thelonious was fortunate enough to be able to pay the bills without resorting to wedding photography or worse, taking "glamour" shots of overweight middle-aged housewives trying to squeeze themselves into sexy lingerie in an effort to put some spice back into their marriages. Not that he'd be hired for these gigs, considering his physical limitations, which was probably just as well. The fact that Thelonious could simply up and go as if life were an endless holiday was one of the things he felt eternally grateful for. Photojournalism jobs were not easy to come by. If he did a good job on his "real Norfolk" assignment, who knew where it might lead? He could end up travelling the world—and not having to pay a penny for the privilege!

Thelonious allowed himself a moment to fantasise about all the exciting and exotic places he could go, documenting each location with a series of photographs that told a story in a way that words could never achieve. He'd been lucky that his unique photographic perspective had caught the attention of a few editors and, more recently, an American publisher of what the Yanks called "coffee table books." And there was talk of more to come, featuring Thelonious behind the viewfinder, provided he could deliver the goods. Apparently this publisher was keen on locations that were slightly offbeat, particularly those that had been successful in maintaining a sense of character and authenticity while everything around them turned into one giant McDonald's. Norfolk was reported to be one of these places, and he looked forward to experiencing a return to the England of the past.

Thelonious congratulated himself on having avoided an assignment in a big city such as Paris or Rome or New York, which would have been a complete misery for someone of his size and stature to work in. Crowds, traffic, noise, being trodden on at every turn—no, that wasn't the most conducive environment for his art, nor was it for living, which was why he'd decided to say good-bye to London and take his chances, letting the cards fall wherever. He could now look forward to peace and quiet, fresh country air, quaint village pubs, and plenty of local ale. He didn't give a toss about the bright lights and the not-so-bright inhabitants of big urban centres. Thelonious had had enough of it, not to mention enough of the crime and grime that accompanied it. Who knows, if he liked Norfolk enough, he might decide to make it permanent. The city was no place for him. Being vertically challenged was difficult enough in the best of circumstances, and living in London was not the best of circumstances. He'd gone through hell as well as great expense getting his Mini Cooper properly outfitted so that he could drive it, because no way was he getting back on the public transport merry-go-round, no matter how much the green fanatics tried to burden you with guilt for driving a car. Why, the last time Thelonious had taken the tube he'd nearly been trampled to death! And don't even talk about the bus. His right leg was still giving him gyp from when that huge Zimbabwean woman had sat on him. Had she not been so busy jabbering on her mobile phone, she might have seen him occupying the seat. But that was London for you: lots of jabber, nothing much to say.

Norfolk. Now that was the *real* England. They didn't even have a motorway. Lots of farms, lots of villages, lots of pubs, but no motorway. Perfection.

It was time to get back on the road, so Thelonious began the arduous process of climbing back into the Mini, wishing for an easier way to get in and out of the vehicle than hoisting himself up and down via the special pulley contraption that had been fitted to the driver's side. Settling himself behind the steering wheel, he reached up to readjust his deerstalker hat over his oversized ears, then punched the specially rigged button on the dashboard to start up the car. The little engine kicked into life, as did Charlie Parker in the CD player. Thelonious's wide foot stretched out toward the raised accelerator pedal, which always felt too far away no matter how many times he kept having it readjusted. Grasping hold of the steering wheel, he manoeuvred the Mini back out onto the B road, heading toward his first port of call: the sleepy village of Little Acre.

Chapter One

LITTLE ACRE WAS ALL ABUZZ WITH news about the murder of one of their native sons. Derrick Pickles, long-time proprietor of The Black Stag public house in the adjacent village of Kelton Market, had been found bludgeoned to death. Pickles had lived in the village since the day he was born, the pub having been in his family for generations. He'd taken it over from his father, who'd taken it over from his father, and so on and so on. The Pickles family were a Norfolk institution, and Derrick was well-liked and respected in the community. Not even the taint of his only son going off to work in The City rather than positioning himself to one day take over the reins of the family business could dampen the locals' affection for the family, though forgiveness wasn't always as easy to come by. Feelings and memories ran deep in this part of the world, despite young Pickles's defection to London taking place nearly two decades before, which, at least to the locals, might as well have been yesterday. Not even the death of his mother many years later could bring young Pickles back in line. But old Derrick stubbornly clung on, running the pub long after most publicans would have sold up and retired to Spain or Portugal—especially a widower with no one to stay behind *for*.

Being the only pub in the village, The Black Stag was a magnet for the locals, not to mention tourists in search of some local colour. Kelton Market was conveniently situated in the county, what with the ruins of an old castle located just outside the village and a bustling crafts and antiques market taking place on weekends, so it was a rare day, indeed, when the pub wasn't busy. The fact that a murder had been committed was not something the residents of this part of Norfolk were accustomed to. The most crime they ever got was of the sort involving the theft of a cockerel from a farm or some youths out joyriding on a tractor. But murder? No. Murders happened in London and Birmingham and Glasgow. They did *not* happen in Kelton Market.

Therefore when Thelonious heaved open the heavy glass door of Little Acre's one and only newsagents in his quest to buy a copy of the local newspaper (or as local as he could get), he discovered quite a crowd gathered inside the cramped little shop. A trio of men representing three generations and an elderly woman who had to have been pushing the century mark were gathered in front of the till, talking animatedly and all at the same time, the garrulous din being added to by a frumpy sixty-something woman behind the counter. She appeared to be refereeing the conversation, her heavy arms flapping and waving about as if she were attempting to direct a newly landed plane to an airport gate.

The youngest of the men was dressed in a white beekeeper's suit, the hood of which had been pushed back behind his head. Hair the shade and texture of the round bales of hay Thelonious had seen in the fields of the surrounding landscape kept falling down over his eyes, causing him to reach up to swipe it away, whereupon the same thing happened all over again. He had the open and guileless mien of someone who'd grown up in the country and had little to no experience with big city life. The oldest of the trio had a pickled and world-weary look about him that could only have been achieved from a lifetime of heavy drinking. His deeply creased face was the colour of cured tobacco leaves, his overall appearance untidy and unwashed. He clutched an unlighted cigarette between the fingers of his right hand, the skin and nails stained a sickly yellow-orange from nicotine. Had it not been for his expensive-looking leather jacket, Thelonious might have mistaken him for a homeless man. The third fellow was aged somewhere between the two and, judging by his collar, appeared to be a vicar. He kept trying to get the group to quiet down, his pale palms making circles in the air as if he were washing invisible windows. Instead of having the desired effect, the group became even more animated, as if seeking to exorcise the vicar's fruitless attempts at calm.

The elderly woman to whom no one paid any mind bashed the rubber-tipped feet of her Zimmer frame against the worn linoleum floor until she was in danger of toppling over. Nevertheless, the accompanying staccato of protestations coming from her shrivelled maw continued to fall on deaf ears. Her hunched form looked as if it might crumple into a heap of ancient bones as she slammed the rattling frame of steel to the lino again and again, her grey head bobbing up and down on her withered neck like a nodding dashboard dog. But no matter how much she crashed and banged and spluttered, she could not be heard above her village compatriots, who were determined to get their points across despite the fact no one was listening to anyone.

It didn't take long for Thelonious to determine that something was definitely up—and the headline shouting at him from the front page of the *Walsham Courier* pretty much confirmed it. He pulled a copy out from the news rack and waddled over to the side of the counter, stretching upward on his short legs to hold out some coins to the sour-faced shopkeeper, who abruptly ceased her refereeing to gawp at him. Not that this was unusual—Thelonious got gawped at a lot, especially by people who'd never encountered his sort before. You would think she'd be a bit more discreet when it came to paying customers, he grumbled inwardly, biting back the urge to tell her to get a new front door fitted. The one she had weighed as much as a London bus. His right shoulder was beginning to ache something awful from the impact of it against the glass when he'd pushed it open. He hoped the B&B his publisher's UK office had booked him into had a bathtub and decent hot water system so he could have a long soak later, because he didn't fancy looking elsewhere for accommodation, especially at the beginning of the summer tourist season. For him to be able to work, he needed a home base, a sense of order. Chaos was not Thelonious' style.

With newspaper in hand, he made his way out of the newsagent's, only to pause outside to examine the cards and notices that had been placed in the shop window (which apparently cost each poster the princely sum of five pounds a week to display). He was curious as to what kinds of items and services people put on offer in these Norfolk villages and expected to see advertisements of either an agrarian nature or for church jumble sales. Not surprisingly, they were positioned too high up for him to read properly, but he did manage to make out a card for an electrician slash handyman as well as a flyer for a beekeeping school before his neck threatened to join his shoulder in protest.

Thelonious trundled back to where he'd left the Mini, climbed up onto the driver's seat with the usual fanfare and aggro, then set off down the little high street with its requisite tea shop/café, gift shop, post office (closed due to government cutbacks), and pub, which went by the rather portentous name The Drowned Duck. Within moments he'd reached the Norman church that marked the end of the village high street. It was also the turnoff for Baxter House Bed and Breakfast. *Home at last!*

The B&B's small car park was empty save for an ancient

bicycle with a chewed-up basket attached to the handlebars. Parking in the shade beneath the overhang of a tree, Thelonious began the tiresome process of extricating himself from the vehicle all over again. He should've come here first, parked, then walked over to the newsagent's instead of making more work for himself. By the time he reached Baxter House's front door he was exhausted and ready to collapse into bed, and he very nearly let out an angry roar on discovering that the bell had been set too high up into the wall for him to reach.

Not for the first time did Thelonious rage against his country and its continuing inability to accommodate those challenged by height or disability. It was one of the things that upset him most about London—the shameful lack of lifts and ramps and all the other accoutrements that made life slightly more bearable by individuals who weren't one-size-fits-all or able-bodied. Not that Thelonious wasn't able-bodied. It was a matter of stature (or lack thereof) that caused him difficulty in a world populated by ignorant and inconsiderate giants.

Visions of relaxing in a steaming-hot bath while enjoying a nice cup of tea quickly overrode any concern for politeness. Thelonious began pounding on Baxter House's front door as if he were being pursued by a pack of rabid wolves. Even if it had been unlocked it wouldn't have mattered—he still wouldn't have been able to reach the handle. After what felt like five minutes of steady pounding from his fist interspersed with an occasional kick from his trainer-clad foot, a shadow darkened the window pane set into the door. It was followed by the pleasing jangle of a key in the lock.

Finally.

The door swung inward, revealing a floral-printed mass of humanity that could have been the newsagent's younger sister. The resemblance ended abruptly, however, when the woman's round pink face bloomed into a huge smile that crinkled her eyes, reminding Thelonious of a female Santa Claus. Somehow he couldn't imagine that vinegar-puss who'd sold him his newspaper ever straining her facial muscles into a smile. The woman bent down, looking as if she were about to give Thelonious's nose an affectionate tweak, and he jumped out of reach of her chubby fingers before they could do any mischief. The only thing worse than being stared at as if he'd just flown in from Planet Zorg was being treated as if he were a kiddie's cuddly toy.

Thelonious managed to growl out a few words to indicate that he had a booking for a single *en suite* room, his voice sounding ragged even to his own ears—though to be fair, he hadn't been using it much. He wasn't big on idle chitchat, having found that life was easier if he kept mostly to himself. He hadn't made a lot of friends in London. Well, he hadn't made *any* friends in London, which was another reason why he was so keen to cross big-city life off his list and relocate to the countryside, where he hoped to find people who were honest and genuine and not just out to impress you—people who could actually enjoy themselves without it always being a competition to see who'd fall into the gutter first from drink. Not that Thelonious was a teetotaller by any means. There was nothing he enjoyed more than a pint of real ale, though finding one in a London pub was becoming a challenge, as was finding anyone working behind the bar with a command of spoken English beyond that of quoting the price of a pint, especially in the more touristy areas of central London, which was often where he had an assignment.

Mrs. Baxter, proprietress of Baxter House B&B, showed Thelonious upstairs to his room, assuring him that it had been recently redecorated by her husband and herself, adding with a saucy wink that she'd put him in the one with the nicest view. The room was also located on the second floor (the topmost one) and required a considerable number of stairs to reach. Despite this inconvenience, Thelonious, after undertaking the arduous trek up into the stratosphere of Baxterland, found himself won over by the uninterrupted vista of rolling wheat fields leading to a windmill in the distance. Or at least he was won over once he'd clambered up onto a chair by the window so that he could actually *see* the view. After all the driving and in-and-out from the car, he was definitely going to need that hot bath, not to mention a nap before venturing out to The Drowned Duck, where he'd decided to spend the evening. Aside from the convenience of being able to walk there, it looked like the perfect place to begin his introduction to Norfolk village pubs. He could hardly wait for his first pint of Norfolk real ale!

As Thelonious scrutinised the chintz-covered twin bed and pondered the prospect of bedbugs, he noticed the framed image of Queen Elizabeth II holding court directly above it. The Baxters appeared to be quite the royalists, for he'd observed in the entry hall a number of photos and knickknacks related to the present Monarch and her family, though he hadn't expected the Baxters' affection for the British Royal Family to extend to the décor of the guestrooms. He supposed it could be worse—Prince Charles could've been ensconced above the bed rather than dear old mumsy.

Thelonious indicated his approval of the room, though he did wonder just how "recent" this so-called redecoration had taken place. The Queen's photo had been taken at least fifteen years ago. Returning downstairs with Mrs. Baxter, he signed the guest register and provided an imprint of his MasterCard (he'd be invoicing his publisher for the full amount once his assignment was completed). With that bit of business out of the way, Thelonious enquired with the usual embarrassment he experienced on such occasions whether it might be possible for a chair to be left outside the door to his room so that he could reach the lock and handle. Not that this solved the problem of the B&B's front door. Thelonious reckoned he'd better not have any late nights or he'd be summoning the Baxters from their bed—and if they were heavy sleepers, he'd be kipping in the car for the night.

Since Baxter House wasn't exactly five-star accommodation, he knew it was unlikely anyone would help him upstairs with his luggage and camera gear, especially Mrs.

Baxter or her husband (who hadn't yet made an appearance). Since there didn't seem to be any other staff, Thelonious trudged back outside to the Mini, where, with some effort and a lot of grunting, he managed to pull his suitcase out from behind the driver's seat. Experience had taught him that this was a more accessible storage area than the boot, which required a bit of a boost-up to reach. Mrs. Baxter stood framed in the doorway like a cherubic matron, beaming as he dragged his expensive case through the gravelled car park, stepping aside and holding open the door so he could re-enter the house. She reminded him of all those supermarket cashiers who sit behind the till picking their noses while the customers struggled to pack their purchases into flimsy plastic bags, delaying the queue of exasperated shoppers behind them. It was no wonder Thelonious had resorted to ordering his groceries online.

By the time he'd finished climbing up the two flights of stairs with his suitcase, the only thing Thelonious felt capable of managing was a nap. He dragged the chair from the window over to the side of the bed, hauled himself up onto it, threw back the duvet, and dropped fully clothed into bed, where he spent the next two hours snoring peacefully and dreaming of sunlit fields of golden wheat.

Chapter Two

THE DROWNED DUCK WAS SURPRISINGLY busy for a village pub on a weeknight. Thelonious scurried through the door after some other patrons, who stopped to gawp at him with the usual stares of astonished disbelief. He trundled past them to a small table in the corner, tossing his deerstalker hat on top to stake his claim lest they got any ideas about commandeering the table for themselves. He examined the chalkboard menu on the wall, the crick in his neck from constantly having to look up at everything and everyone inspiring him to hasten the selection process. Sod's Law they'd be out of what he wanted. That always happened when he had his chops watering for a specific dish.

Having decided, Thelonious made his way over to the bar to place his order, hoping that no one would step on him or trip him up before he got there. He couldn't wait to try some proper Norfolk ale. He just hoped the Goth-chick barmaid would notice him, since he wasn't about to put himself through the indignity of climbing up onto a stool to reach the bar and her multi-pierced ear. She wasn't at all what he'd been expecting in a Norfolk barmaid. Camden Town, yes, but not in what amounted to a one-horse village in rural Norfolk!

Earlier when he'd awakened from his nap, Thelonious had taken a hot bath, which had been a struggle to climb in and out of, splashed on his favourite cologne, and changed into fresh clothes. He was fortunate in being able to pack light when he travelled, his garments not requiring much space or being too heavy inside his little suitcase. The downside of being small in stature was that he had to shop in the children's department—and the humiliation of this was so great that he preferred to just shop online, taking his chances that his purchases would fit. It wasn't easy finding clothes in his size range that didn't have pictures of giraffes or the Teletubbies on them, and Thelonious often had to opt for the more expensive "designer" lines, which at least produced clothing that looked as if it had been intended for miniature adults rather than shrieking red-faced tots.

Sometimes he wondered whether he should go the bespoke route and be done with it. Not that he had money for such extravagances as custom-made apparel. And even if he did, where did he go that required more than the casual wear he already owned? It wasn't like he hung out at trendy London bars and nightclubs or ate in fancy restaurants. In fact, Thelonious couldn't even remember the last time he'd had a night out. It was just too much bother and embarrassment, and he never met anyone worth talking to anyway. Even his local had become a place to avoid, especially after the pub over by the council estate had shut down and its denizens, having no place else to go to get pissed, decided to frequent *his*. To say they were a rough lot was no exaggeration. Thelonious didn't fancy being tossed about like a football by a bunch of hooligans!

Although he'd only been in Little Acre a few hours, most of which he'd spent unconscious on his bed, Thelonious already recognised some of the patrons in The Drowned

Duck. Holding court at the bar was the booze-marinated fag smoker he'd seen at the village newsagent's. Despite the warm temperature inside the pub, he continued to wear his leather jacket. As Thelonious drew nearer, he was forced to conclude from the sour smell emanating from it that the fellow never took the thing off. He was drinking whisky and chatting to another familiar character—the wheat-haired young man in the beekeeper gear, his drink of choice having just been pulled by the Goth barmaid.

An older man carrying a dead pheasant in one hand emerged from behind a pair of swinging doors leading to the kitchen. He joined in the conversation, his expression grave. Thelonious kept hearing the name "Pickles" being mentioned and reckoned they were discussing the murder of that publican that had been in the newspaper. Since this recent contributor to the discussion was very likely The Drowned Duck's publican, it was no wonder he didn't look too cheerful. Nor, for that matter, did the pheasant, which was as dead as the unfortunate Mr. Pickles.

Although wanting to eavesdrop more, Thelonious's empty belly overrode his curiosity and he ambled over to the side of the bar where there was more chance of being noticed by the barmaid. The beekeeper politely stepped aside to allow him to pass. Thelonious expected to be treated to the requisite gawp of disbelief, but the lad appeared not in the least bit fazed. He even offered a friendly smile before returning to his conversation with Fag-stain Man and the pheasant-wielder. Thelonious was feeling in better spirits already, especially when the barmaid hurried over to take his order, her smile indicating that she found him kind of cute. London suddenly seemed very far away, and he was itching to immerse himself in Norfolk life.

Thelonious had originally planned to order the local pheasant, but he didn't like the look of that road kill the publican was waving about, so he opted for the safer route with fish and chips, which was fresh local cod in a crispy beer batter, plus a side order of Norfolk's famous samphire—a regional plant that grew in the tidal marshes and which someone with too much time on his or her hands had discovered was quite tasty when steamed, then sautéed in butter. Aside from fish, Thelonious liked pretty much anything that grew from the ground.

"Sure you don't want a shandy, mate?" quipped Fag-stain Man as Thelonious's pint was being pulled. "That ale's strong stuff." His tobacco-cured face broke into a wide grin, displaying an abundance of nicotine-stained teeth that matched the skin on his fingers.

Thelonious shot the man a dirty look as he accepted his pint from the barmaid. Although this wasn't the first time he'd been the recipient of these kinds of comments, he thought it best to ignore them. Turning away from the bar, he carefully made his way back to his table, clutching his first pint of real Norfolk ale as if it were liquid gold. The rubber soles of his trainers stuck to the old wooden floor with each step and he wondered what he could have stepped in, since he'd walked straight to the pub from the B&B, not gone wandering off into a field full of cowpats. Setting the glass down on the seat of his chair, he climbed halfway up, relocated the pint to the table top, sat down, and returned his deerstalker hat to his head. The barmaid would be bringing his food order over, so at least he didn't need to clamber back down any time soon.

As for the matter of his trainers, with his rotten luck he'd find them smeared with fresh dog shit, which would be a nightmare to clean off, not to mention disgusting. The last time it happened, Thelonious had ended up chucking his shoes in the bin rather than dealing with the muck from some filthy cur's backside. Not that he had anything against dogs, providing they kept their distance. Unfortunately, they didn't always keep their distance, especially when their ignorant owners let them off their leads. Thelonious had barely escaped with his life that time he'd gone to enjoy a sunny summer afternoon in a neighbourhood park. He'd contacted his local MP immediately afterward, demanding that the laws for sex crimes be extended to include canine perpetrators. Nothing ever came of it.

Thelonious turned up each foot to discreetly investigate the soles of his trainers. Rather than the catastrophe he'd been expecting, he discovered that they were coated with a substance that had the look and consistency of honey. How he could've stepped in honey was an even bigger mystery than the dog-poo scenario, and he shot a puzzled glance at the beekeeper, trying to form a link between him and the shoes. The lad hadn't shifted an inch from his place at the bar, nor had his nicotine-stained companion, whose whisky glass was in the process of being replenished by the pheasant-brandishing publican. There was something familiar about the older man. It was as if Thelonious knew him from somewhere, though he couldn't for the life of him think *where*.

As he waited for his food to arrive, Thelonious, bored with reading and re-reading the chalkboard menu, decided to check out the other patrons in the pub, only to recognise yet another face. At a nearby table was none other than the peacekeeping vicar from the newsagent's. Although Thelonious expected vicars to be a fairly sober lot, this particular vicar was downright funereal. He sat at a table, staring morosely into his pint glass. A drab-looking woman of indeterminate age occupied the chair across from him, staring with equal melancholy into her glass of white wine. Judging from the lack of conversation, eye contact and sexual chemistry, Thelonious assumed she was the vicar's wife.

A trio of thirty-something Belgians occupied the next table over, their "Red Devils" football shirts a dead giveaway of their nationality, as was the fact that they were speaking in French. As for the bottles of Stella Artois they were drinking, Thelonious would have thought they'd have better taste, coming from a country that produced some of the finest beers in the world. There was something a bit off about the three men. They kept glancing around nervously as if they believed they were being watched, only to return to a huddle, their heads almost touching as they continued to talk amongst themselves. Thelonious was probably imagining suspicious behaviour where none existed—until he noticed that the men really *were* being watched.

Their observer, a balding jowly fellow in his mid-fifties who could've done with the loss of a stone or two, was seated at a table near the door, reading a copy of the *Walsham Courier* that had the Pickles murder emblazoned across the front. The newspaper obscured most his face, though his eyes peered over the top of the page to study the three men. *Real subtle, mate*, mused Thelonious, downing a satisfying swig of ale. The man's keen interest in the Belgians seemed out of place in a village pub located in the middle of farm country. To their credit, the Belgians weren't bad looking, if you went in for that sort of thing. As for the attention they were getting from the lone newspaper reader, perhaps Little Acre was a Mecca for cottaging, in which case Thelonious made a mental note to avoid all public conveniences during his stay.

His pint was going down a real treat, just as he knew it would. Thelonious found himself being lulled into one of those "all is right with the world" moods, and it was heightened when the Goth-chick barmaid passed by and gave him a wink, which he returned. He chuffed with laughter as he wondered if the ancient Zimmer-frame lady would come hobbling into the pub next or maybe even Mrs. Baxter with her husband. Thelonious had seen her on his way out that evening, but had not seen Mr. Baxter, despite the landlady informing him in a pointed tone that Thelonious had only just missed him coming in from the garden. Considering that the window in his room looked straight down into the garden and it had been empty of human habitation before he'd gone downstairs, Thelonious didn't consider Mrs. Baxter's claim too plausible. It seemed odd that she felt it necessary to mention her husband in the first place, especially when he hadn't asked after him. Did she think he had designs on her? Thelonious might not be every woman's cup of tea, but surely he could do better than the floral-printed bulk of Mrs. Baxter!

While Thelonious continued to contemplate the romantic

and highly deluded machinations of the B&B's landlady, a mangy dachshund suddenly appeared among the tables. It waddled from one patron to the next, begging food, its sluggish movements indicating that it was quite advanced in age. Not having any luck, the creature eventually found a chair to its liking (which also happened to have one of the Belgians seated on it) and began to hump one of the back legs. Apparently there was still a bit of life left in the old boy, despite his obvious decrepitude. The Belgian whose chair it was shifted forward in the seat, as if this would place him safely out of the line of fire.

"Lord Nelson! Get back here right now!" The pheasant-wielding publican chatting with Fag-stain Man and the beekeeper came out from behind the bar. Setting the dead bird down alongside the beekeeper's pint glass, he clapped his hands together sharply to get the dog's attention. Lord Nelson, pausing from his seduction of the chair leg, stared myopically at his owner before putting forth a few more humps for good measure. Abandoning his quest for pleasure, he waddled over to Thelonious, at which point the air quality in the pub took a distinct turn for the worse. The mangy old mutt had farted.

Lord Nelson looked up at Thelonious, his thin black lips curving into a smug grin. Thelonious glared down at the dog and growled, which had no effect. Lord Nelson moved off in his own sweet time, nearly tripping up the Goth-chick barmaid, who was bringing over Thelonious's food order, its long-anticipated arrival sullied by the boiled-cabbage effluvium that had now taken up residence in Thelonious's nostrils courtesy of Lord Nelson. The mutt trotted back to his owner with a new spring in his step, as if he'd just taken a dose of doggy Viagra.

Smell or no smell, Thelonious was famished and he tucked into his fish and chips as if he'd spent the last few months in hibernation, interspersing it with bites from the buttery samphire, the branches of which he ate in their entirety rather than filtering the softer bits through his teeth.

He realised he was making a lot of noise while he ate, but he couldn't help the fact that he chomped his food. He made quick work of it all and had already moved on to studying the dessert specials listed on the chalkboard when he had the uncomfortable feeling he was being watched. Shifting his gaze to the right, Thelonious found it being met by an inquisitive stare from the heavyset fellow seated near the door. Considering that he could've read his newspaper a dozen times over, it was no wonder he had nothing better to do than spy on the customers. Maybe he'd grown bored after the departure of the Belgians, who'd left the pub in the interval between Lord Nelson's potent fart and the arrival of Thelonious's food order.

The man hoisted himself up out of his chair and came straight over to Thelonious's table, pint in hand. The fact that the glass was almost full worried him, especially if this character was looking to chew the proverbial fat over a pint. "Take it yew enjoyed your meal?" The intruder's jowly face contained an expression of amusement that didn't sit too well with Thelonious, nor did the overly familiar tone accompanying it.

Thelonious managed to nod in affirmation, hoping this would be the end of what was probably an innocent attempt to make a visitor feel welcome. This was Norfolk; it stood to reason that here in the country the locals would be more open and friendly.

The man stuck out a beefy hand, waiting for Thelonious to accept it. "Detective Chief Inspector Horatio Sidebottom of the Norfolk Constabulary Criminal Investigations Department," he introduced in a whoosh of beer-scented breath. A smile fixed itself to his broad farmer's face. Thelonious didn't find it reassuring. Out of everyone in the pub, why should a Detective Chief Inspector randomly single him out for conversation?

Thelonious's heart sank into his recently filled gut. As far as he was aware, idle pub chit-chat did not generally extend to full introductions that included job titles, particularly long-winded ones. It could be that the inspector was simply showing off, expecting to impress this latest tourist to pass through the village. Although Thelonious enjoyed his television police dramas as much as the next fellow, he preferred to steer clear of any involvement with law enforcement, especially since he'd had to fudge some numbers pertaining to his height in order to get his driving licence.

The silence stretched uncomfortably, though the DCI's smile didn't waver. Someone had to give in, and it was obvious which of the two it would be. "Thelonious T. Bear," said Thelonious when it seemed he had no recourse but to reply, accepting the proffered handshake with trepidation. His vocal cords felt creaky, which came from not using them much. It embarrassed him that nearly everything he said came out in a growl—not that this was any fault of his. He was lucky he'd even developed the capacity to speak, considering....

"Just passing through our little hamlet?" Despite his jocularity, DCI Sidebottom's words held an undercurrent that told Thelonious he had no business being here.

Thelonious shook his head. "I'm staying here," he croaked in response, suddenly losing all desire for that sticky toffee pudding with custard he'd seen on the dessert menu. If this was an example of welcoming tourists to the area, Thelonious felt about as welcome as diaper rash on a baby's backside!

Sidebottom's unkempt eyebrows shot up to his balding pate, and he leaned an elbow on the table, further invading Thelonious' space. "Is that so?" The smile had vanished. He stared hard at Thelonious as if he'd just announced his intention to steal the crown jewels. "Yew staying at Mrs. Baxter's then?"

With a choking cough, Thelonious forced down a bit of samphire that still lingered in his throat, wondering why he felt guilty when he hadn't done anything wrong. No wonder the Belgians had been behaving so strangely what with this

Sidebottom character breathing his beer-fumes down their necks. "How did you know that?"

"Nowhere else in the village to stay," Sidebottom answered with a chortle. "How long yew here for?"

"A few days." That was a lie. It was more like a few weeks, but the DCI didn't need to know that. Since Thelonious would be travelling all over the county in search of interesting photos to take (and availing himself of as many pubs as possible), the odds of running into the inspector again didn't seem that high.

"Mind if I join yew?" Without waiting for an acceptance, DCI Sidebottom claimed the chair opposite, plonking his pint glass down onto the table as if staking his territory, which, in effect, he was. He continued to scrutinise Thelonious for signs of anything suspect. "Big fan of the Monk then?"

It took a moment for Thelonious to realise what the inspector was talking about. Before he could formulate a response, Sidebottom provided clarification, speaking slowly as if to someone mentally challenged. "Thelonious Monk? The famous jazz musician?"

Thelonious knew full well who Thelonious Monk was. He took pride in his knowledge of classic jazz, not to mention his mental ability—he didn't need to be spoken to like the village idiot. Nevertheless, he held in his anger, not wanting to create trouble where none existed. "I'm more a fan of the Bird," he replied tersely.

"Ah...Charlie Parker." Sidebottom nodded in agreement. "Good stuff, that."

Since the comment didn't require an answer, Thelonious didn't provide one. However, his silence did little to deter the inspector, who appeared determined to engage his unwilling audience in conversation at any cost. "Music hath the power to soothe the savage beast."

Breast, you fool! Thelonious wanted to shout, the urge to correct the DCI on his misquote almost as strong as the urge to be rid of him. But he reckoned that the less he responded, the more likely it was the inspector would get bored and be on his way. At least he hoped so.

"Do a bit of Morris dancing myself," continued Sidebottom, "when I can manage the time."

Thelonious was unable to imagine the cumbersome detective chief inspector participating in anything that required coordination and skill, not unless that coordination and skill consisted of emptying pints down his gullet. That beer gut he sported had to have originated from *somewhere*.

"What's with the 'T'?"

Thelonious just stared, once again completely lost in the meandering drifts of the inspector's discourse. Did the man suffer from attention deficit disorder? Because his comments and questions didn't follow any logical pattern—or at least none that Thelonious had been able to determine.

"The '*T*'?" repeated Sidebottom, his expression indicating that he thought his drinking companion wasn't exactly the brightest button in the box. "In your name? Just wondering what the 'T' stands for, is all."

This time it was Thelonious's turn to feel stupid, but how was he to know what the DCI was on about? It appeared the inspector wasn't giving up until he knew everything, including Thelonious's blood type. By going to the village local for a pint and a meal, he'd unwittingly placed himself on the conversational hit list belonging to a bored policeman. He let out an exasperated gust of air, the sticky toffee pudding he'd had his heart set on an unfulfilled fantasy. He'd never be able to enjoy it with DCI Sidebottom's fat backside parked at his table.

Thelonious cleared his throat to speak, the result sounding like a Harley Davidson motorbike starting up. "'Teddy.'"

The inspector cupped his ear with his hand. "How's that?"

"The 'T' stands for 'Teddy'!" repeated Thelonious more loudly than he'd intended. The vicar and his wife turned to gawp at him, as did Fag-stain Man and the beekeeper from over at the bar. Even the deceased pheasant seemed to be taking a sudden interest…until Thelonious realised that the publican had propped the carcass up on the bar in an attempt at humour.

Satisfaction suffused the inspector's face as if he'd just solved the crime of the century. "That explains it, then."

"Explains *what?*"

"Well," Sidebottom leaned across the table conspiratorially, "you're not exactly a typical Norfolk tourist, are yew? Though I imagine you're not a typical tourist *anywhere.*"

Thelonious's irritation sparked thoughts of a primitive blood-thirsty nature the likes of which he'd not experienced since he was a cub and hadn't yet developed the ability to control his more animalistic instincts. He must've looked ready to tear out Sidebottom's throat because the inspector held up a chubby palm as if to stave off a blow. "Whoa there, Ted! No offence intended! It's just that we don't get a lot of bears round these parts." He let out a large guffaw. "Deer, pheasants, jack rabbits…but I've yet to meet a bear."

"Well, you've met one now."

"So I have, so I have." Sidebottom leaned back in his chair as if settling in for a nice long evening—in which case he'd be spending it alone, because Thelonious was out of here.

Choking down the last of his ale, Thelonious made a move to indicate he was ready to leave. Besides being annoyed with the inspector, he was knackered what with all the driving he'd done today and climbing up and down Mrs. Baxter's stairs. He wouldn't have been at all surprised to find that they'd multiplied in number since he'd gone out, Mr. Baxter having added on a few extra just to make life more difficult for guests on the second floor.

Thelonious yawned pointedly, prompting DCI Sidebottom to pull farther back in his chair until it looked ready to tip over. He knew he had an impressive set of choppers in his mouth, which no doubt accounted for the inspector's sudden lack of companionability. A few moments passed in silence, giving Thelonious hope for an escape. Just as he began to climb down from his chair, Sidebottom spoke, causing him to almost miss his footing on the chair rung. "Expect yew heard about that murder over in Kelton Market." The DCI shook his head grimly, his eyes never leaving Thelonious's face. "Derrick Pickles was a good man. A shame, that. A real shame."

Although he felt called upon to say something respectful in acknowledgement, Thelonious had nothing to add; after all, it wasn't as if he'd known this Derrick Pickles.

"We don't get murders round these parts," the DCI continued. "Tends to be fairly quiet other than occasional sheep rustling or theft of farm equipment or a spot of bother with the Gypsies. Bloody travellers! More often than not you'll find *they're* behind any trouble here." Sidebottom gave Thelonious another of his hard stares. "When was it yew arrived in Little Acre?"

Thelonious didn't like where the conversation appeared to be heading, but he thought he'd better answer. Not to answer would make him look as if he had something to hide. "This afternoon."

"Drove in, did yew?"

His nod elicited a derisive snort from the inspector. Thelonious wouldn't have been surprised if the DCI hadn't already run a vehicle check on his car. Well, his record was clean. He didn't have so much as a parking violation!

"Stop anywhere along the way?"

"Not really."

"Well, either yew did or yew didn't. So which is it?"

Thelonious was definitely starting to worry. Did Detective Chief Inspector Sidebottom have some kind of a quota?—and was *he*, as the stranger in town, the most viable suspect for any crimes that had been committed within the last 24 hours? All Thelonious could think about was his bed back at the B&B and how much he wanted to be tucked into it. In his distraction he answered with more force than he should have. "I drove straight here from London!"

Sidebottom's posture stiffened and he leaned forward in his chair, no longer intimidated by Thelonious's earlier display of teeth. "There's no call to get testy, *Ted*."

"I'm not getting testy!" roared Thelonious, his claws extending as if in readiness to attack. Thankfully the publican chose that moment to clang the bell, shouting for last orders, the flatulent Lord Nelson barking in accompaniment.

The inspector chugged down what remained of his pint, setting the glass on the table with a grunt of pleasure. "Well, I'd best be off or the missus'll have my guts for garters." He pushed himself up from the chair. "Expect I'll be seeing yew around then."

Thelonious shrugged his furry shoulders, hoping for the opposite.

"Yew take care," Sidebottom called out as he reached the door. "And don't go leaving Little Acre without saying goodbye!"

The eyes of everyone in The Drowned Duck were on Thelonious, including those belonging to the flirtatious barmaid. Even Lord Nelson kept cutting suspicious looks in his direction in between licking his backside. Thelonious wanted to crawl beneath the table and hide. Was this DCI Sidebottom's subtle way of telling him not to leave town?

Waiting until he was certain the inspector was long gone from the vicinity, Thelonious clambered the rest of the way down from his chair and left the pub. His gait felt unsteady as he made his way along the deserted high street toward Baxter House. Maybe Fag-stain Man had been right about the local ale being strong stuff. Good thing he hadn't opted for a second pint or he'd be confessing to a murder he didn't commit, not to mention confessing to every murder in the county's history, including those that had taken place before he was born. That would've made Detective Chief Inspector Horatio Sidebottom's day for sure.

As Thelonious had feared, the B&B's front door was shut and very likely locked. Although he'd been given a key, it was useless. He couldn't reach the keyhole, let alone the handle to open the door. He looked around for something to drag over to the door to stand on, but the only thing he saw that could be of any use was a large ceramic pot containing the dying remains of a plant—and it was cemented to the front stoop. Did Mrs. Baxter actually think someone was going to steal it? Clearly something needed to be done about the situation. He couldn't go through this every time he returned from being out. The lightweight foldable metal stepladder he always kept in the car boot for these kinds of emergencies had been stolen the last time he'd bought petrol and he hadn't had a chance to get a replacement. He'd been inside buying some sweets and when he came out, the thing had vanished. His folly not to have packed it back into the boot first, but he'd only been gone a minute!

Thelonious hammered his paw against the door, hoping someone inside the house would hear him because if not, he'd end up sleeping in the Mini. It hadn't even gone past eleven—surely the Baxters weren't in bed already? He waited for what felt like a reasonable length of time for someone to come. When nothing happened, he put his paw back into action, this time with more force. Just as he resigned himself to a restless night spent in the Mini's back seat, a shadow blocked the light showing through the pane of glass in the door. It was followed by the sound of a key turning in the lock. The door opened inward, revealing a satiny pink confection of a dressing gown with Mrs. Baxter's head protruding from the top. The garment reminded Thelonious of a chewed piece of bubble gum.

"Why, Mr. Bear!" Her broad face lit up as if Colin Farrell had appeared at the door armed with a bouquet of red roses. Thelonious trundled past her into the reception area, his mood foul. "I suppose we should sort something out so that you don't have to ring the bell every time you come back from a night out."

A night out? The woman made it sound as if he'd been out clubbing, not down at the village pub, from which he'd returned before the clock had barely struck eleven. He was on the verge of telling her that if he'd been able to ring the bell, he might also have been able to reach the keyhole, but was too exhausted from his encounter with DCI Sidebottom of Norfolk CID to bother. Instead he clomped up the never-ending stairs to his room, grateful to at least find the chair he'd requested waiting for him, though it was too far away to be of use and he had to drag it down the corridor to his door. Thanks to the ale he'd drunk and the samphire he'd eaten, Thelonious was bursting at both ends for the toilet, and it was all he could manage to climb up onto the chair and get his door unlocked before more pressing needs demanded his attention.

Thelonious lumbered across the carpeted floor, his short legs propelling him to the bathroom in record time. He hopped up onto the toilet seat and got himself settled, gazing absently into his room through the open doorway. The Queen watched him from her place of honour above the bed, a slight smile on her lips. The irony of sitting on the throne before Her Majesty Queen Elizabeth II was not lost on him, and at any moment he expected to hear a rousing chorus of "Rule, Britannia!".

No sooner did he flush the toilet than there came a tapping on the door. "Mr. Bear?" Mrs. Baxter called through the closed door. "Is there anything else I can get for you tonight?"

Thelonious, suddenly remembering that he'd neglected to lock the door, hauled up his trousers as if a pack of starving wolves were after him. The thought of the landlady walking in on him in the toilet was not something he wished to experience. He launched himself at the bed and scrambled up onto it, whereupon he began to let out an exaggerated series of snores. When the tapping came a second time, followed by a tentative "Mr. Bear?", he upped the volume, throwing in a few hearty snorts for good measure. A moment later he heard the creak of the old floorboards. He envisioned Mrs. Baxter's pink-satin bulk moving off down the corridor and away from the sanctity of his room.

If Baxter House Bed and Breakfast was offering late-night room service, Thelonious didn't want what was on offer.

Chapter Three

Bow, East London
VINNIE AND DESMOND CLARK LAY sprawled across the sofa as if someone had thrown them there. The brothers were making quick work of the tins of lager Vinnie had just bought down the off-licence on the high street—the off-licence with that sour-faced Paki at the till, Abdul or whatever the fuck his name was. Vinnie couldn't stand the geezer and was convinced he had it in for him, always making a big song and dance out of checking and rechecking his twenty-pound note as if he'd printed it off himself and the ink was still wet. Pikey bastard. What was a Paki doing selling booze anyway? Shouldn't he be peddling dodgy curries that gave you the shits for a week? Vinnie thought Pakis weren't allowed to deal in booze. Or maybe that only applied to drinking the stuff, not selling it. Seemed no one had any values these days.

The light from the flat-screen television reflected off the brothers' matching shaved skulls, both of which were a landscape of lumps and bumps and scars—souvenirs from various run-ins and scuffles over the years. They wore them with pride, Vinnie especially, preferring to display the evidence of their toughness instead of hiding it beneath hair. They reckoned since they were both prone to male pattern baldness like their old man, it was better to shave it all off rather than look like one of them sorry tossers with a receding hairline. Besides, the birds thought a shaved head was sexy. Not that Vinnie needed any help in *that* department. He considered himself a ladies' man and made a point of shagging as many fit birds as possible without actually catching something. Desmond was a bit more tight-arsed about that sort of thing, though his brother vowed to cure him of that.

The Clarks' washed-out blue eyes were glued to a satellite broadcast of West Ham playing the Spurs on their brand new high-definition widescreen telly that hadn't fallen off the back of a lorry, but instead came from a fancy electronics shop on the high street. Nowadays only the best was good enough for the brothers, especially Vinnie, who pretty much made all the major decisions in the household. Hell, they had enough money to pay for it. They had enough money to pay for a whole shed-load of tellies, providing they had a shed to put them in. The Clark brothers were moving up in the world, no doubt about it.

That job they'd done up in Norfolk had been child's play—easiest bit of dosh they'd come by since getting out of the nick last year. Till now they'd been lying low, wanting to keep the Old Bill off their necks, but it was time to get back into business—and get back into it in a big way. It'd been destiny that hooked them up with that posh git from Chelsea. Vinnie had sized him up real good, tacking on the equivalent of VAT to their bill and then some, all of which went into the Clarks' pockets. The dozy toff had accepted their terms without batting an eyelash. Now *that* was class!

The Clarks had it made. They had it *so* made they could've changed their surname to Riley, as in "the life of." They rented their terraced house on the cheap from the Council, laughing their arses off at the stupid tossers who paid through the nose to rent or buy one of those new-build cubby-holes in the area. Ever since that first whiff of the Olympics, house prices and rents had been skyrocketing, bringing in all the London yuppie scum who suddenly thought it was cool to live east of the river. Guess their eyesight was so bad from all the wanking they did that they couldn't see the grim tower blocks with the clapped-out lifts from the safety of their posh little balconies. Not that the Clarks were complaining about the change in demographics. They loved it—those trumped-up city boys were easy pickings. You could always count on a Rolex watch when you mugged them.

Desmond hauled himself up from the sofa, stretched, scratched his balls, and headed off to the kitchen to sort out their tea. They were going to have one of those poncey microwaved ready-meals from Paolo Louis Black, that big shot ginger-haired celebrity chef on the telly. Vinnie would've preferred something nice and greasy from the local chippy, but his brother was always rabbiting on about how they needed to make themselves more upmarket, especially now that they were moving in posher circles. As far as Vinnie was concerned, that new geezer they did jobs for hadn't hired them for their sophisticated taste and table manners. He just wanted the job *done*.

As Vinnie contemplated taking a quick toilet break before his brother brought out their meals, a powerful slam shook the house, followed by voices arguing loudly in Polish. The neighbours had come home. The ruckus continued from the hallway on into the lounge, which shared a wall with the Clarks. It was impossible in these old terraced houses *not* to hear your neighbours, but there *were* limits. Finally Vinnie couldn't stand it anymore. He leapt up from the sofa and went for the wall. "Shut it, ya fuckin' pikeys!" he shouted, banging his fist against the paper-thin structure separating the houses. Its surface already bore the marks of earlier poundings—any more and the two properties would become one.

"Oi!" yelled Desmond from the kitchen. "What the fuck ya doin'?"

"It's them fuckin' Poles again," Vinnie yelled back, giving the wall one final thump with the meat of his fist. "One of these days I'm gonna kill—"

Desmond appeared in the kitchen doorway, drying his hands on a tea towel. He'd seen it all before. His brother's temper was nothing new to him, nor was being the one to try to put a balm on it. "Vinnie, remember, we don't do freebies no more. From here on it's strictly professional. We're proper businessmen now."

"Yeah, yeah," grumbled Vinnie, returning to the sofa and the football match, which was giving him a right hump thanks to the cock-up from West Ham's goalie that put the Spurs closer to victory. He hated the fucking Spurs. He hated them even more than he hated fucking Crystal Palace.

The Clarks' neighbours had moved off to another part of the house to continue their domestic squabbling, leaving Vinnie to stew over the game and the misfortune of having a bunch of pikeys living next door. Every day it was the same thing—the Polish geezer yelling at his wife and whacking her about. One of these days he was going to kill her. Can't say Vinnie'd blame him—she looked so thick he'd have been willing to off the stupid cunt himself if it meant getting a bit of peace and quiet.

Why didn't these spongers go back to where they came from? Worst thing that ever happened to this country was joining the European Union and opening up the borders to these freeloading foreign scum. Vinnie's politics were BNP all the way and he was proud of it. Britain for the British. British jobs for the British people, not a bunch of Poles or Eye-Ties or Africans, who weren't even *in* the fucking EU, so what the fuck were they doing over here in the first place? Bad enough his tax money was being pissed away on building fancy superhighways in Spain—now it was supporting all these hubu-jubu benefit scroungers from the bush!

Well, if he actually *paid* any tax, that is.

"Oi!" shouted Vinnie in the general direction of the kitchen. "Are we ever gonna eat? I'm fuckin' starving 'ere!"

"Keep your hair on!" Desmond shouted back. A moment later he appeared in the lounge carrying two plates, both of which contained a microwaved carton and a fork. He handed one to his brother, whose wide flat nose wrinkled with distaste. "Shoulda gone down the chippy," he grumbled.

"Come on, Vinnie, it ain't that bad," replied Desmond, reclaiming his spot on the sofa.

Vinnie made a big show of sniffing the contents of the steaming carton. "Smells like puke," he said, poking his fork into it and shovelling a chunk of asparagus cannelloni into his mouth. His stained and misshapen teeth mashed it to a pulp, which he swallowed. What the fuck, he was hungry. He reckoned he could always go down the chippy later and get some *real* food. "Tastes like puke, too," he added with a burp.

"At least it's free."

"If I wanted free, I'd get meself banged up again at Her Majesty's pleasure."

Desmond couldn't argue with that. Though he hated to admit it, these posh ready-meals did kind of taste like puke. But he'd never say that to his brother. Bad enough Vinnie always thought he was right about everything. Why make life harder by encouraging him?

The brothers gulped down the rest of their asparagus cannelloni while West Ham lost the match.

Chapter Four

AFTER A GOOD NIGHT'S KIP, THELONIOUS felt right as rain the next morning. Thankfully there'd been no more return visits from Baxter House's landlady, though he still made certain to lock his door, even going so far as to block it with the chair for extra security. Not that he considered himself a hunk, but it didn't do to take chances, especially if Mr. Baxter had gone underground as he was beginning to suspect. Mind you, if Thelonious was married to Mrs. Baxter, he'd go underground, too!

All of a sudden he felt guilty. The woman was only trying to attend to her guests' needs, which was what any good B&B landlady should do. Thelonious was ashamed of himself for having such uncharitable thoughts. Maybe he'd been living in London for too long and had become suspicious of everyone's motives, not to mention jaded. He needed to relax and unwind and let his creative juices flow. He had a job to do, a publisher to please, and a new life to start. And what better place to do so than right here in Norfolk?

The previous night's encounter with DCI Horatio Sidebottom at The Drowned Duck now seemed like something out of an episode of *Midsomer*. In the clear light of day Thelonious could have a good chuckle about it. As with Mrs. Baxter, he had overreacted by thinking the worst. Being tired and stressed from the long drive, he'd read things into the situation that weren't there. Granted, the inspector *had* been nosy, if not outright annoying, but that didn't make him guilty of police harassment.

He couldn't help wondering if every visitor to the village ended up on the receiving end of DCI Sidebottom's cross-examination style of pub chitchat. Perhaps that accounted for why the car park at Baxter House was empty save for a broken-down old bicycle and his Mini Cooper—word had gone out to avoid Little Acre because it was inhabited by a busybody policeman who liked to chew the fat with tourists! Well, at least the B&B was quiet. Thelonious wouldn't have been able to stand it if the place was overrun with screaming children or rutting couples on a romantic getaway in the English countryside.

Thelonious resigned himself to keeping Baxter House as his home base for the duration of his assignment, since everything was pretty much to his needs—or as near to them as possible. The chair in the corridor seemed to have become a permanent fixture outside his room, and just this morning he'd discovered a wrought-iron version placed strategically by the B&B's front door. Providing no one moved them, his problems with locks and door handles were solved. Mrs. Baxter might've been a bit of an oddball, but at least she was bothered enough to accommodate her guests' special needs. He still hadn't seen any sign of Mr. Baxter, but at breakfast his name was mentioned so often by his wife that Thelonious felt as if he'd known the fellow for donkey's years. Perhaps it was all this clean Norfolk air and summer sunshine, but he couldn't remember feeling this good since…well, he couldn't remember when!

For his first official day in the county, Thelonious decided to meander northward in the direction of the coast, stopping hither and thither, then wrapping things up by taking some beach shots in the late afternoon, providing the weather didn't turn foul or the wind so fierce that he'd be whipped to death by the sand. The stuff played havoc with his fur, not to mention his camera lenses. If all went well, he should get some good photos, especially once the sun wasn't so intense that it bleached the colour out of everything. He couldn't leave it too late though, since he'd heard the Wash at high tide could be deadly. Thelonious didn't fancy being swept out to the North Sea, only to wash up as a fur ball on some beach in France or Belgium. In the meantime, he'd stop at whatever location caught his fancy along the way, take a batch of photos, then reward himself with a hearty lunch starring a pint of real Norfolk ale in a traditional Norfolk pub in a charming picture-postcard Norfolk village. Now that was the life! He could already see his future playing out before him, just one perfect day after another.

Thelonious punched the button for the car stereo, which was pre-loaded with a Charlie Parker CD, and "Birdland" filled the speakers. He whistled along as fields of wheat rolled gently past, the sunlight turning the stalks to gold. London seemed a million miles away with its noise and grit and roads choked with cars, buses and taxis. The fresh country air whooshing into his nostrils through the Mini's open windows was making him peckish and he wondered if he'd last till midday before needing to stop and eat. Mrs. Baxter's breakfast (which he'd had to rush downstairs before 9 A.M. to eat) hadn't exactly been the last word in *haute cuisine*—unless *haute cuisine* had suddenly become raggedy slices of toasted white bread with butter substitute, undercooked bacon that had been previously frozen, overcooked eggs, tinned beans and tinned tomatoes. Thelonious had assumed that out here in the country he'd be getting a freshly cooked breakfast rather than bits and pieces that had been sitting around all morning in a metal warming tray and whose origins were highly suspect. There wasn't so much as a kipper in sight—and he adored fish of every kind, kippers especially. At least the cup of tea was tolerable (barely), though admittedly it would be difficult to get wrong the placing of a teabag into a pot of hot water. Mind you, the milk did taste a bit off. Well, he'd make up for it at lunchtime.

Thelonious spent the morning and early afternoon pulling off the road to capture the rich golden light as it washed over the wheat fields and round bales of hay that made up the landscape, unconcerned as to whether he might be trespassing on someone's farmland. Since he didn't see any fences, he figured he was safe. The only living thing that seemed to object to his presence was a pesky hare—and a few pointed growls eventually sent it packing. The sun provided Thelonious with some dramatic light and shadow compositions, which were further enhanced by the low angle of his shots. His creative juices were definitely boiling on a high flame today—a fact that was confirmed each time he checked the viewfinder to examine the photos he'd taken. He hadn't been this excited about his work in a long time, and he took it as a sign that he should seriously consider making his home here.

The rumbling from Thelonious' stomach threatened to overtake the more melodious tones coming from The Bird. He had to eat—and he had to do it *soon*, because he was starting to feel cranky. His temper always took a nosedive whenever he was hungry. Not that this was unusual for his kind, but when you lived among humans, it was wise to take preventative action before problems arose. This was a lesson many of his ursine *compadres* hadn't yet learned, which explained why so many didn't function well in their adopted society and ended up returning to the wild.

A white signpost appeared up ahead, indicating the names of several villages, all of which were in opposite directions. Slowing down to determine which road might take him to the nearest one (and to food), Thelonious suddenly found himself being assaulted by the unexpected blare of a horn. So startled was he that he jumped in his seat, banging his knee on the steering wheel. The rear-view mirror showed a black Audi right on his tail, its driver clearly in a big hurry to get somewhere. Thelonious thought he'd left all that rushing about nonsense back in London. Someone must've neglected to inform the Audi's driver that this was a rural road in Norfolk, not the Westway!

Thelonious opted for the village of Hunters Cove. According to the car's SATNAV, it was in the same direction as the Wash, which fit in with his afternoon plans for the beach. It sounded like the perfect place to soak up some good old-fashioned Norfolk ambiance, along with some good old-fashioned Norfolk ale. The name conjured up high seas and swashbuckling pirates and hidden treasure. Thelonious could feel the inspiration already and was itching to get behind the viewfinder. He'd take some quaint village-y shots after lunch—that would give the ale a chance to wear off before he got back behind the wheel. Considering the difficulty he'd had in obtaining his licence, it wouldn't do to get pulled over for drunken driving. Though maybe his new best friend Detective Chief Inspector Horatio Sidebottom could pull a few strings should that happen, he mused with a chortle, envisioning the busybody inspector bailing him out of jail.

Putting his strength into his short arms, Thelonious turned the Mini Cooper's steering wheel to the left, not bothering to signal his intentions to the driver of the Audi, veering onto a small road that promised to take him to Hunters Cove in two miles. Of course, two miles on a small country road could often feel like the equivalent of ten miles anywhere else. Nevertheless, Thelonious wasn't disappointed as the wheat fields and hay bales gave way to a picturesque little road lined at both sides with terraced cottages made from a distinctive pebbly stone. This eventually gave way to a high street filled with shops featuring the same facade. Thelonious had arrived at his destination.

Hunters Cove was several times more bustling and vibrant than Little Acre and offered far more in the way of shopping, including a very upmarket art gallery as well as several boutiques that would've looked more at home in London's Primrose Hill than a small hamlet in the Norfolk countryside. The village even had the equivalent of a lunchtime traffic jam, which further reminded Thelonious of the empty state of his belly, since he now found himself stuck in the midst of it. If he didn't eat something soon, he'd start gnawing on his arm. He couldn't help noticing the large number of expensive cars either idling in traffic or parked along the kerb. There was definitely some serious money in Hunters Cove.

Suddenly Thelonious was forced to jam his wide foot down onto the upraised brake pedal when a convertible BMW shot out in front of him from a side street, having just run the stop sign. He was rewarded for his quick reflexes with the loud blast of a car horn and he glanced irritably in his rear-view mirror, seeing a familiar-looking black Audi behind him. The vehicle was so near that he could make out the London residential parking permit stuck to the windscreen.

As the traffic inched along, Thelonious debated whether to look for parking or cut his losses and go elsewhere. But if he tried to stave off starvation a bit longer and opt for someplace less busy, it was possible the pubs he came to would've stopped serving lunch by then. These places in the sticks tended to be quite militant about their food-service hours—and there was always the danger of them running out of the most popular dishes even if you found one still serving. There was nothing worse than having your chops all set for a nice steak and kidney pie, only to be told it had sold out. You'd think these publicans would know what their popular items were and have enough on hand to accommodate the demand. The only pubs with open-ended food service hours and a never-ending supply of it seemed to be those that dished out that cheap and nasty frozen rot they bunged into the microwave—and Thelonious wasn't about to throw away good money on something he could buy at his local Tesco for a third of the price.

No, he was here now and here he would stay—there couldn't be this amount of traffic congestion if the village had nothing to offer hungry visitors. Just because he hadn't seen any pubs didn't mean they didn't exist. Whoever heard of a village without a pub? Yet with each minute Thelonious spent stuck in traffic, his despair grew and just when he finally accepted the fact that Hunters Cove had no relief for his empty belly, the Mini managed to scoot up a few notches, bringing into view a pub with the pastoral moniker The Pheasant Inn. The place looked old and it definitely looked Norfolk—he was certain the publican had a pint glass with his name on it!

Forty minutes later Thelonious made it through the pub's front door. It had taken him that long to find a place to park. He'd probably burned several litres of petrol between idling in traffic and circling the village again and again until someone finally vacated a parking space. And he'd nearly lost it too, since it turned out that the obnoxious driver of the black Audi shared the same goal. They'd both been driving on the same narrow side street from opposite directions when a silver Lexus pulled away from the kerb, freeing up a parking spot. Although Thelonious was closer *and* on the correct side of the road, the Audi decided to pull a fast one and moved to cross over from the other side of the road to claim the empty space. Well, Thelonious wasn't having it. He jammed his foot down onto the upraised accelerator pedal. With a screech of rubber, the Mini shot forward, slotting itself neatly into the opening and nearly colliding head on with the Audi as its driver endeavoured to do likewise. The now-familiar horn sounded and Thelonious let out an angry roar in response, baring his teeth at the driver, who executed a quick reverse manoeuvre and sped off down the street. Thelonious felt well pleased with himself and reckoned his little victory might be worthy of *two* pints of ale instead of one.

The Pheasant Inn boasted a large and sunny patio at the back. Being such a fine afternoon, Thelonious decided to eat outside. He loved being in the fresh air—a commodity that was difficult to get in the city. He hoped he'd find an empty table, since it was still the lunchtime rush and everyone probably had the same idea. As it turned out, there were a handful of unoccupied tables. Unfortunately, the pathways leading *to* them were obstructed by noisy throngs of young men and women standing about with pints of lager and glasses of white wine respectively.

Their voices sounded out of place and unpleasantly shrill in the wholesome Norfolk sunshine. Clearly, they weren't locals. They looked as though they'd been transported from a trendy wine bar in Sloane Square onto the back patio of a Norfolk village pub. The groups were posed like wax figures in a display at Madame Tussauds, providing Madame Tussauds actually *did* displays of Chelsea yuppies. Thelonious figured they were tourists up from London doing the exact same thing here that they did there. It made him wonder why they bothered to leave home.

The concept of *al fresco* dining lost its appeal. Even if he commandeered one of the vacant tables, Thelonious wouldn't have been able to move his arms to eat due to the crush of bodies pressing in on him from all directions. To make matters worse, the reek of fag smoke hung over the entire area and he didn't fancy getting it into his fur or, for that matter, his lungs. He was a staunch non-smoker and hated the stench of the filthy things. The best thing that ever happened was when the British government finally grew a pair and brought in the no-smoking ordinances in public places. Before then just walking into a pub was like a date with the Grim Reaper.

Thelonious resigned himself to eating inside rather than being subjected to the air pollution and peacock-like displays of self-importance from the patio denizens. At least he wouldn't have the view of their backsides while he ate, which would've put him right off his food, not to mention turned his ale bad. This was exactly the sort of thing he'd wanted to get away from, and he was surprised to come upon it in

Norfolk of all places!

Pulling his deerstalker hat down over his ears, Thelonious went inside The Pheasant Inn and headed for the bar, which was separate from the main section of the pub, which was really more so a restaurant. As he waited for someone to appear and take his order, his glance fell upon the incongruous presence of a glass humidor of Cuban cigars sitting out on a display table. Cuban cigars in a Norfolk village pub—now didn't that take the biscuit! It seemed the county was full of surprises, not all of them pleasant. If anyone dared to light up one of the foul things while he was in the vicinity, there'd be hell to pay.

Thelonious returned his eyes to the bar, where they were met by those of a young barmaid, who glared down at him as if he were cow dung she'd stepped in. If she could be any more up herself she'd be serving pints out of her backside, he mused, wondering if she even *knew* how to pull a pint. In a low rumble, Thelonious asked to see a menu (no chalkboard version being in evidence), his growly voice made more so by his discomfort. Maybe he should've taken the lack of parking in the village as an omen and gone elsewhere.

"We stop serving in ten minutes," snapped the barmaid with a scowl. She leaned forward over the bar to hand him a menu, giving every indication that she was very put out for having to do so. The menu was still several feet too high for Thelonious to reach and he had to climb up onto a stool to get it. As he hurriedly perused the pub's culinary offerings, she kept a suspicious eye trained on him as if she expected him to steal one of the expensive Havanas from the humidor.

According to the menu, The Pheasant Inn was owned by Paolo Louis Black, the famous ginger-haired celebrity chef who was always on television. He was also always in the headlines of every tabloid in the country, all of which reported in salivating detail his antics as an adulterer and womaniser. Not that Thelonious read such tripe, but it was hard to avoid hearing about the man. Black was usually seen with a silicone-breasted collagen-lipped bimbo on each arm—

girls so young you'd expect them to still be wearing their school uniforms were it not for the hard-core cosmetic enhancements. Black was evidently suffering from a case of midlife crisis no doubt made worse by fame and the money it brought. The fact that his wife hadn't left him was probably due to the fact that the chef was loaded and rumoured to become even more loaded if his recent foray into the ready-meal market proved successful. Every major supermarket chain in Britain was selling his microwavable meals—and at more than twice the cost of competing brands. Shoppers were grabbing them up as if the end of the world were approaching, apparently unconcerned that they were being ripped off. Well, not Thelonious. He refused to buy glorified TV dinners, no matter how glorified the packaging or whose name was printed on the box!

The Pheasant Inn had no pheasant on the menu. After the road kill the publican at The Drowned Duck had been waving about the night before, this wasn't a huge disappointment to Thelonious. What *would* be a disappointment was the absence of Toad-in-the-Hole, Mixed Grill, Cottage Pie and all the other hearty pub fare he'd been gnashing his chops over since morning. There was grilled filet of sea bass with fresh greens. There was couscous with mussels in a tarragon and leek sauce. There was even something called Norfolk Bouillabaisse, which, according to the description, was a patented dish of Paolo Louis Black's. But when it came to proper pub grub, the menu came up empty.

When Thelonious noticed the prices listed alongside each dish, he almost roared in protest. Why, he could've bought three Charlie Parker CDs for the price of the sea bass alone! If this was the lunch menu, he'd need to sell his Mini Cooper if he hoped to afford dinner. Annoyed, desperate and hungry, he opted for the cheapest thing on the menu—a burger, which would set him back a cool fifteen quid. Though tempted by a side order of buttered samphire, it would've run him nearly the cost of *one* Charlie Parker CD, so he decided to give it a miss. To think that he could have driven not even ten minutes to the salt marshes and picked the stuff himself. Thelonious couldn't believe the nerve of this Paolo Louis Black character charging that kind of money for something you could get for free—and which cost pennies to prepare. He was definitely in the wrong business.

Thelonious gave his food and drink order to the snooty barmaid. After paying and waiting an eternity for her highness to pull his pint of ale (which she did *not* fill to the brim), he opted for a small table in the corner of the bar area, preferring this location to the noisy dining room, which would've necessitated him having to tack on a tip for table service. It wasn't that he was cheap, but after being gouged for a humble burger he didn't feel inclined to be generous in the gratuity department. He also didn't want to eat to the accompaniment of the braying voices that were carrying over from the dining room. The Sloane Square contingent had come in from the patio. Having done their best to contaminate the fresh air outside, they probably wanted to do likewise to the inside air, ponging it up with the residue from their nicotine addiction.

Once again Thelonious concluded that all the time and energy he'd put into finding a parking space had been a sign that he should've gone elsewhere. But he couldn't have faced dealing with the hassle all over again in another village, along with the whole in and out of the car business, especially on an empty stomach. Going anywhere beyond the confines of his own home always felt like more trouble than it was worth, though he'd be damned if he let the world beat him down. Besides, he was technically homeless. He'd given up his flat and was now going to get out there and explore the world. Things could only get better from here.

Hauling himself up onto a chair, Thelonious felt the barmaid's eyes boring a hole into his back. If there hadn't been the risk of her gobbing into his food, he would've given her his best effort at a two-fingered salute. Instead he seethed in silence, drinking his ale, which tasted as if it had come from a barrel in serious need of being changed. After a wait of forty-five minutes, his burger finally arrived, delivered lukewarm courtesy of a spotty-faced lad whose service style consisted of dropping the plate onto the table, which caused several of the chips to tumble off onto the table top. Thelonious wondered when anyone had last cleaned its surface, a cursory swipe with a dirty rag not being his idea of proper food-service hygiene. Mind you, those fake fingernails on that barmaid didn't inspire confidence in the pub's sanitary practices either.

By now Thelonious was hungry enough to tuck into the kid's leg, and after he saw what was on his plate, he regretted not giving the matter more serious consideration. Perhaps they'd mistaken him for a rabbit? Though he couldn't imagine any rabbit finding much here to sustain life. A whole-grain toasted bun camouflaged the diminutive patty of beef that passed for a burger. This was tarted up with an accompanying sprig of rocket lettuce and some bits of shredded carrot so few in number that Thelonious could have counted them on one paw. The chips, which had been done French style and cut so thinly as to be almost transparent, lay scattered around the burger in an attempt to make the dish look artistic. Instead it emphasised the fact that their portion, much like everything else he'd been given, was just plain measly. A miniature pot of Paulo Louis Black's famous mango chutney (also available in major supermarkets) vied for space in this barren and depressing landscape.

Thelonious sighed miserably. He would need a second lunch after this gastronomic feast if he hoped to rid himself of the vacancy in his belly.

By the time he left The Pheasant Inn, there was little sign of the summer sun he'd initially planned to have his lunch beneath. In fact, it looked like rain. At some point between the beer garden yuppies and the Cuban cigars Thelonious had lost all desire to take any photos in the village and really just wanted to be on his way, having wasted enough valuable time already. Perhaps he should've taken a photo of that ridiculous lunch he'd been served and sent it in to *Ripley's Believe It or Not!*, because frankly, Thelonious still could not believe it.

On his way to the car, a gust of wind nearly blew his deerstalker hat clear off his head. Thelonious barely managed to grab hold of it before it went sailing down the high street, probably to end up trodden on by the 21st century Sloane Rangers. Back inside the Mini, he fitted the hat securely onto his head, tucking his ears beneath the rim as much as it was possible to do. Suddenly he heard the beeping of a horn. Another vehicle, a silver Mercedes, was waiting to claim his parking spot. Seemed like Hunters Cove was as busy as any village in London. He'd be glad to see the back of it.

Thelonious drove in the direction of the Wash, hoping that the wind off the North Sea would blow away the ominous-looking rainclouds by the time he reached the beach. The weather in Britain, especially near the coastlines, could be unpredictable, which was one reason why he made certain to factor in plenty of extra days for assignments, since it wasn't unheard of for him to be stuck indoors reading a novel while he waited for the weather to clear. Of course, he sometimes got his most dramatic shots after the rain had been and gone and the sun had started to emerge from behind dark clouds. But there wasn't much call for photographing grey murk.

Just as he pulled into the car park at the beach, a drizzle began to fall. Thelonious's planned late-afternoon stroll with his camera instead became a quick toddle to the water's edge for a few hurried photos, followed by an even quicker toddle back to the Mini as the drizzle turned to full-on rain. Hauling himself up onto the driver's seat, he yanked the door shut, his damp trousers squelching unpleasantly against the built-up cushion that had been permanently attached to the upholstery. There didn't seem to be much point in trying to wait it out; high tide was due to arrive and Thelonious didn't fancy trying his luck with underwater photography. As he sat there contemplating his next move, he noticed an orange plastic envelope affixed to the windscreen of the car.

A parking ticket.

He couldn't believe his rotten luck. Not that he was trying to dodge paying for parking, but the truth of it was he hadn't been able to reach the pay-and-display machine. Thelonious would need to buy another foldable metal stepladder and soon before he encountered any more problems. Since he hadn't expected to be at the beach for very long what with the rain kicking in, and considering the fact that everyone was driving *out* of the car park rather than driving into it, he reckoned he'd be fine. It had already gone past five o'clock when he'd arrived, which left not even an hour before the parking became free. What were the odds of a parking warden being around at this time of day—*and* in this weather?

Thelonious was fuming. Had the service at The Pheasant Inn not been so appalling, he might've made it to the beach while there was still some decent weather left instead of arriving in a downpour—*and* with high tide threatening to sweep him away. Now he had a parking violation and imminent pneumonia. Water dripped in a slow torture from Thelonious's ears onto the scruff of his neck, creeping beneath his shirt collar. He shook his furry head, sending droplets flying in all directions. It had been his folly to leave his trusty deerstalker in the car, but he'd feared it would get blown off in the wind and he doubted he'd be lucky a second time. He sneezed, then sneezed again. That Paolo Louis Black had a lot to answer for.

Snorting with irritation, he high-tailed it out of the car park and back onto the main road, the Mini's windscreen wipers doing double duty as they sent the orange plastic envelope soaring off into a rain-shrouded wheat field. Until now Thelonious had always been a decent law-abiding citizen, but this parking ticket business was taking the piss.

He arrived back at Baxter House in time to be accosted by Mrs. Baxter, who was lurking on the upstairs landing near his room. Armed with a feather duster, she appeared to be in the process of dusting the door handles. "Why, Mr. Bear, I was hoping I'd see you!" she cried gaily, her flowered housedress looking considerably shorter than he remembered. Either she owned the exact same garment in several lengths or she'd just spent the afternoon taking up the hem. If the latter, Thelonious didn't even want to think about her reasons for doing so.

All at once she stooped down to his level, looking as if she were about to pinch his nose, her broad face registering concern. "Goodness me, you'll catch your death if you don't get out of those wet clothes!"

Thelonious took several steps back, not liking the unwholesome gleam in the landlady's eyes. He was perfectly aware of being soaked through. And he was perfectly aware that he needed to change out of his clothes into something dry. But if Mrs. Baxter was hoping to assist him with the task, she had another think coming. Had the blasted woman not been so determined to waylay him, he'd be soaking in a hot bath by now instead of standing in the corridor dripping cold rain onto the carpet.

"I put some more teabags by the kettle in your room," she said. "And some biscuits. A nice cuppa and you'll be right as rain!"

Considering he'd just been rained on, Thelonious didn't appreciate the sentiment. Nevertheless, he grumbled his thanks and was about to climb up onto the chair to unlock his door when Mrs. Baxter removed a key from the pocket of her housedress and proceeded to perform the task herself. "There you go, Mr. Bear! Thought I'd save you the bother since I'm already here!" Thelonious pushed past her into the room and was about to shut the door when it was blocked by her floral-printed bulk. "Is there anything else you need?" she asked, the hope in her voice striking genuine alarm in him.

Thelonious pressed his weight firmly against the door, expecting the landlady to take the hint and shift out of the way. Surely she wasn't making a play for him? Though he had nothing against older women, Mrs. Baxter wasn't his type. For one thing, she'd probably roll over in her sleep and crush him to death. For another, she was married—and he didn't fancy being on the receiving end of her husband's fist. Providing, of course, she *had* a husband. Thelonious had seen neither hide nor hair of the famous Mr. Baxter and was beginning to wonder if he even existed. Perhaps the landlady had invented him in the event the B&B's more criminally minded guests wouldn't think that she was a woman on her own and take advantage of the situation by emptying the house of its valuables. Not that there seemed to be anything of value in the house, unless you were a collector of cheap tat relating to the Royal Family. The thought of anyone taking advantage of Mrs. Baxter in a more intimate manner never crossed his mind. It was more so likely to be the other way around. Indeed, Thelonious feared for the safety of any fit young male burglars who might find their way into Baxter House B&B.

"I'll bid you a good night then," said Mrs. Baxter, sighing with disappointment as she removed herself from the doorway. Thelonious could hear her sighing all the way down the stairs even after he'd shut the door.

After a hot bath and a brief lie-down, he returned to The Drowned Duck, where at least he knew he wouldn't get his pocket picked for a meal. Besides, it was the only place in the village open in the evenings, the tea shop/café being a lunch kind of establishment. Baxter House didn't serve dinner. They didn't serve lunch either. Not that Thelonious would've been inclined toward either, having already sampled the culinary delights of one of Mrs. Baxter's "cooked" breakfasts. He hoped things would improve in that quarter, since he was a firm believer in eating a proper breakfast.

The Drowned Duck's quirky charm and unpretentious clientele proved to be just the tonic after Thelonious's experience at The Pheasant Inn—or, as he now dubbed it, The *Unpleasant* Inn. No sooner did he toddle through the door than he found himself being greeted with a smile of recognition from the Goth-chick barmaid, who set about pulling his pint before he'd even reached the bar. Now that was service! Thelonious felt like a regular already, despite the fact that this was only his second visit. He could see himself developing an affection for the pub and making it his local for the duration of his stay.

The young beekeeper was at the bar, engrossed in conversation with Fag-stain Man. Both looked as though they hadn't moved from the previous night, frozen in a moment of time save for the fact that the beekeeper's pint glass and his companion's whisky glass went from full to empty, then back up to full again. Thelonious wondered if the beekeeper slept in that beekeeper gear, since he'd yet to see him wearing anything else. As for the lad's older cohort, his clothes looked as if they could benefit from some soap and water—as did the fellow himself. Fag-stain Man continued to sport his leather jacket, which gave off a rank odour Thelonious detected the moment he'd entered the pub—a rich stew of dead animal and unwashed homo sapien. His sensitive nostrils quivered with distaste; for once he was grateful for his diminutive stature, which made it impossible for him to reach human armpit level.

"No shandy tonight?" quipped Fag-stain Man, serenading Thelonious with a phlegm-enriched laugh accompanied by a brown grin that was even more repellent on the second viewing. Thelonious shot him a dirty look and, tugging his deerstalker hat down over his ears, paid the barmaid for his pint. Ignoring his would-be heckler, he trundled toward the table he'd occupied the night before, more certain than ever he knew the man from somewhere. He only hoped it wasn't from the television programme *Crimewatch*.

The brief journey from bar to table was like walking on flypaper. Each time the rubber soles of Thelonious's trainers made contact with the old wooden floorboards, he felt them sticking to the surface. The floor probably just needed a good clean. Someone had likely spilled their pint and hadn't bothered to alert the staff to mop it up. Good thing he always wore trainers instead of regular shoes, since it reduced the chances of them accidentally coming off. Nevertheless, he clung possessively to his pint, not wanting to lose a valuable drop of it.

Settling himself at his table, Thelonious got down to the serious business of drinking his ale, wanting to make it last until he made a decision about food, at which point he'd order another. Suddenly the identity of the hygienically challenged fellow at the bar came to him. He was surprised he hadn't recognised him before! Fag-stain Man was none other than the lead guitarist in one of the most famous rock bands in the world—a band that had been around since the Sixties and which epitomised the sex, drugs and rock 'n' roll lifestyle. It was a wonder the man was still alive, considering all the substances he'd ingested and injected into his body over the years. Thelonious heard that a few celebrities lived in Norfolk; apparently Fag-stain Man was one of them.

Thelonious kept himself entertained with the nightly rituals at The Drowned Duck. The publican's flatulent dachshund had emerged from behind the bar and was waddling about the room, begging crisps and chips and anything else he could con from the patrons in between humping chair legs and the legs of anyone who remained still long enough to allow him his pleasure. Not wanting to tempt fate, Thelonious drew up his feet to the topmost rung of the chair so Lord Nelson couldn't reach them—not that it would've been possible what with the dog's low height and Thelonious' short legs, but why tempt fate? He was glad he'd splashed on some eau de cologne before heading out for the evening. Although he was always meticulous with his hygiene and grooming (unlike many of his kind, he was sorry to say), a dog could still smell his scent in a room full of human beings, and Thelonious didn't want to take any chances. He had enough to worry about with Mrs. Baxter's raging hormones.

The Belgians sat huddled together at the same table they'd occupied previously. This evening they were joined by a new cast member—a jowly Russian who appeared to possess a fondness for belching. The Belgians spoke to the Russian in French, and he replied back to them in burp-infused Russian. Thelonious kept hoping that someone would turn up the volume of the music being piped in over the pub's sound system so he wouldn't have to hear them—his hope for relief short-lived when The Cure was replaced by Barry Manilow.

He didn't know which was worse—the garrulous quartet at the table or songs that made the whole world sing. Well, Thelonious didn't feel like singing. Even Lord Nelson lost the mood, abandoning the chair leg he'd been happily seducing to go plop down morosely in front of the empty fireplace, where he continued to season the air with his boiled-cabbage effluvium.

A couple of tables away sat the vicar with Mrs. Vicar, neither making any effort at conversation. They raised their glasses to their lips in a mechanical motion, drinking the contents with no indication of enjoyment. The fellow had to be the grumpiest-looking vicar Thelonious had ever seen. It wouldn't have surprised him if the local parishioners never bothered to turn up for Sunday service, what with that dour mug facing them from the pulpit. Not that Thelonious was big on church going. He still had nightmares from his Christmas visit to St. Paul's Cathedral when an Italian tourist nearly crushed him to death as she sat down in the pew, apparently not noticing that he was already there. Fortunately he'd managed to scoot out of the way of her lethal backside in the nick of time. From that point on he vowed to steer clear of major tourist attractions.

Thanks to the strong ale, Thelonious found himself being lulled into a sense of calm and relaxation. If he didn't focus on any one sound, the conversations, clanking glasses and piped-in music blended into a reasonably inoffensive soundtrack, with no particular element overshadowing the other. After the afternoon he'd had, he was finally starting to wind down and was just about to signal the barmaid for another pint when he heard a loud ruckus coming from the pub's front door. It sounded as if someone were trying to break it down with a hammer, or worse, an axe, and he half expected to see a gaping hole filled by the maniacally grinning face of Jack Nicholson shouting "Here's Johnny!". By now everyone's attention was focused on the door. Even the Belgians and their Russian cohort had fallen silent and were craning their necks to determine the source of the disturbance.

The door began to inch open by tiny increments, the widening breach first revealing a silvery flash of steel, then a glimpse of brown cloth. The tension in the room was thick; even Fag-stain Man's glass of whisky had halted in mid-air inches from his mouth. Thelonious could feel the fur on the back of his neck prickling, so caught up had he become in the drama. Something was determined to get through that door, and it wasn't going away any time soon.

Suddenly a limb of ancient flesh appeared in the gap. The vicar jumped up from his chair and hurried over to pull the door open the rest of the way...whereupon the culprit of all this mayhem was finally revealed.

A hunched-over bag of bones crowned with a small grey head came teetering through the doorway, an expression of stubborn determination on its withered features. With each movement forward, the rubber-tipped feet of a Zimmer frame crashed to the floor, coming dangerously close to the vicar's canoe-sized black brogues. The old woman Thelonious had seen at the newsagent's the day he'd arrived in Little Acre clattered into The Drowned Duck, her rheumy eyes fixed on the bar. The vicar continued to hold the door open until she'd managed to clear the threshold, at which point she nodded her thanks, catching the toe of his shoe beneath the rear foot of the Zimmer as she clanged past. He returned to his table and his wife, who glared at him with irritation and, unless Thelonious's ale was stronger than he thought, *jealousy*.

Fag-stain Man's mouth erupted into a brown grin as the old granny ambled at a snail's pace toward him. Within moments a glass of whisky was waiting for her on the bar alongside his newly replenished one. Everyone seemed to be holding their breath, as if to see whether she'd be successful in her quest or keel over midway. Even Barry Manilow had stopped singing—and Thelonious hadn't smelled a fart coming from Lord Nelson's direction in a good five minutes. He noticed that the Belgians had each slapped a five-pound note down onto their table, which was matched by one from the Russian, their attention riveted to the action playing out before them as if they were having a day out at Epsom Downs. Maybe there weren't any horses running today and this was the next best thing, mused Thelonious, wondering if he should get in a bet himself before grandma reached the finish line.

Everyone watched as she inched nearer to the bar, each modest bit of headway resulting in a discordant clang of metal, the NHS-issue Zimmer frame threatening to break apart as it hit the floor. Thelonious hoped she didn't drive a car, because if she did, that pheasant the publican had been brandishing about the night before wouldn't be the only road kill in the area. He cut a quick look at the vicar, who had his left shoe off and was massaging his big toe through his sock, doing his best to ignore the satisfied smirk on his wife's face.

At last the old woman reached the bar, whereupon the Russian shouted "*Za vashe zdorovye!*", scooping up the money from the table and waving it in the air in a celebratory gesture. With a flourish worthy of Lord Byron, Fag-stain Man handed the elderly arrival the glass of whisky, her reward for having accomplished the seemingly impossible feat of making it from the door to the bar. Zimmer-frame Granny tossed it back in one go without so much as a flinch.

Life at The Drowned Duck returned to normal—or at least what passed for normal in these parts, for Thelonious was discovering that what was normal for Norfolk wasn't necessarily normal for anywhere else. Conversations resumed, as did Barry Manilow's saccharine warbling and Lord Nelson's potent farting and the Russian's enthusiastic belching. Thelonious went back to his pint, thinking that he should order some food. He could definitely go for some of that buttered samphire again. As he perused the chalkboard menu to check out the dinner specials (which were the same as yesterday's, including the pheasant), the door opened yet again—and in walked Detective Chief Inspector Horatio Sidebottom of Norfolk CID.

Thelonious's appetite did an abrupt about-face. Apparently the misery of the day had not yet come to an end.

Spying Thelonious seated by his lonesome, DCI Sidebottom took it as an open invitation and barrelled on over to join him. "Ted!" he greeted loudly, as if encountering an old and dear friend. Thelonious cringed. Anyone within a fifty-mile radius of The Drowned Duck had to have heard him. Even Lord Nelson, who up till now had been enjoying a well-earned rest from humping chair legs, raised his head to offer Thelonious a black-lipped grin. If Thelonious didn't know better, he'd think the mangy cur was laughing at him.

Sidebottom parked his lumpy posterior on the spare chair opposite. "How yew keeping?"

Bristling at the inspector's overfamiliarity, Thelonious grumbled something noncommittal in response. Although he didn't want to overreact again, he hoped his lack of enthusiasm might inspire the man to seek out another drinking companion. As before, the DCI wasn't taking the hint. "How's the holiday?" he asked, waving at the barmaid, who waved back in acknowledgement and began pulling his pint.

Thelonious hadn't actually said he was on holiday. In fact, he'd never said much of anything, other than admitting that he was staying locally. His reasons for being in Norfolk didn't seem worth explaining—not that they were any of the inspector's business. Photojournalist bears probably didn't exist in DCI Sidebottom's limited world of stolen tractors and Gypsy sheep rustlers. Mind you, there *was* that murder in the neighbouring village....

As if reading his mind, the inspector stared sharply at him, adding: "Hope all this murder business hasn't put yew off our fine county?"

For some inexplicable reason the words struck fear into Thelonious's gut. He knew he was being silly—Sidebottom was simply making a random comment to a newcomer, as anyone might when something so horrible had taken place. Yet the words hung between them like Lord Nelson's bad pong, saying something else—something that was giving him cause to worry.

"Norfolk born and bred myself," said the DCI after receiving no response.

An annoying itch had begun to make itself known above Thelonious's left ear, and it was growing worse with each moment the inspector remained at his table. When he tried to wedge his paw beneath his hat to scratch, he almost knocked it off his head. He decided to suffer rather than endure the indignity of climbing down from his chair to fetch the deerstalker off the floor, only to climb back up again—and do so in front of an audience. As the itch continued to plague him, Thelonious wondered if something had crawled into his hat and set up shop there. His first thought was fleas, and he shot Lord Nelson a deadly look. The mangy mutt was sound asleep, snoring and farting by the hearth. That only left bedbugs, which sounded even worse. Thelonious made a mental note to check under the mattress when he got back to his room.

"Never seen anything like it," said Sidebottom, shaking his head. "We don't get murders round these parts."

The inspector seemed to be observing Thelonious in a way that indicated he was expected to confess to the killing right then and there. Thelonious felt like asking how Derrick Pickles could have been murdered when they didn't get any murders "round these parts" but decided to hold his tongue. It would only draw suspicion to himself, though he'd done nothing suspicious—unless coming to Norfolk qualified as *suspicious*.

The Goth-chick barmaid delivered Sidebottom's pint to the table; apparently the fellow was planning to stick around for a while. As for Thelonious, he just wanted a quiet pint and some food. Now, rather than being left in peace, he could look forward to being under the close scrutiny of Lieutenant Columbo for the rest of the evening. He supposed he could head back to the B&B and see if Mrs. Baxter might be inclined to fix him some sandwiches, though the prospect didn't sound too appealing, if her breakfasts were an indication of her culinary skills. Thelonious could envision the sandwiches already: doughy white bread filled with a paper-thin slice of some unidentifiable cheese, a rancid sprig of lettuce, and a pigeon-turd's worth of Branson's pickle. If he were *really* lucky, the cheese might be accompanied by a transparent slice of ham only a few days past its sell-by date. The alternative would be to go elsewhere to eat, which would mean leaving the environs of Little Acre—and Thelonious didn't fancy driving around in the pitch blackness of rural Norfolk until he stumbled on a pub or restaurant still serving food, especially after drinking on an empty stomach.

That was all he needed—a drink-driving charge on his record. He'd gone through hell getting his full driving licence and was very nearly rejected until he kicked up a fuss about discrimination on the basis of disability, citing "little people" as an example of others who were vertically challenged, yet still legally allowed to drive. Thelonious disliked having to call attention to himself, but sometimes he had no choice. After all, nobody else was going to stand up for his rights!

DCI Sidebottom drained his glass in one go and leaned back in his chair with an expression of smug satisfaction, as if emptying an entire pint glass filled with beer down his gullet without taking a breath was an achievement on a par with being awarded the Victoria Cross. Although Thelonious had long ago owned the fact that he wasn't the last word when it came to table manners, he'd never understood this male proclivity for swilling down pints—which tended to go hand-in-hand with falling over into the gutter afterward.

"When was it yew arrived in these parts again?" queried the inspector, glaring at Thelonious' scratching paw as if expecting it to pull a gun out from under the deerstalker hat.

Thelonious hadn't been aware that he'd started scratching again and he thrust his paw guiltily beneath the table, hiding it from Sidebottom's view. "Yesterday," he croaked, sounding like a convicted felon even to his own ears.

"And where did yew say you're staying? Baxter House, was it?"

Considering that Baxter House was the only accommodation in the village and considering that they'd gone over this the night before, Thelonious wasn't too impressed with DCI Sidebottom's savvy police methods. If he was in charge of the Derrick Pickles murder investigation—which he seemed to be—the odds of it being solved were about as good as Lord Nelson availing himself of some Wind-*eze* tablets. Mind you, the way things were headed, the inspector would get Thelonious banged up for the killing—and be promoted to superintendent for having made such quick work of it.

Oh, why hadn't he stayed in tonight? Thelonious berated himself. Would it have hurt him to go without dinner for once? It wasn't as if he couldn't spare the loss of an inch or two from his waistline. The DCI looked in no danger of running out of conversation, reminding his captive audience that their evening together was only getting started. "Mrs. Baxter...such a lovely woman," the inspector sighed, his farmer's features softening and taking on a whimsical expression.

A lovely woman?

Thelonious almost fell off his chair. He wanted to ask if there was another Mrs. Baxter in the village, for surely Sidebottom couldn't be referring to the one from the B&B. Apparently Little Acre was a hotbed of unbridled lust and romantic intrigue, with the buxom proprietress of Baxter House at the core. Well, Thelonious wanted no part of it. As soon as he got back to his room he'd drag the bedside table in front of his door in case the woman took any funny turns during the night and showed up in his bed.

Sidebottom, suddenly noticing his pint glass was empty,

began to raise his hand to signal the barmaid for another, then evidently thought better of it. "Never had anything like this happen, especially not on my watch."

Thelonious had to hand it to him—in the blink of an eye the inspector had switched topics, moving from the not-so-obvious physical charms of Mrs. Baxter to the brutal bludgeoning to death of local publican Derrick Pickles. Perhaps this was all part of a strategy to confuse him and trap him into a confession. Thelonious felt a loosening in his bowels as he waited for Sidebottom to clip the cuffs on him.

"Well, I'd best be off home to the missus." The inspector's chair scraped the wooden floor as he hefted himself out of it. "She's made us a Cottage Pie."

Thelonious could feel his chops watering. That had been one of the dishes he'd expected to find on the menu at The Pheasant Inn, and his stomach began to rumble in Pavlovian earnest as he imagined the jowly inspector tucking into the mash-covered mince in its rich brown gravy.

DCI Sidebottom delivered his empty pint glass to the bar and, after offering a jovial handshake to Fag-stain Man and the beekeeper, returned to Thelonious, clapping him hard on the shoulder as if they were old drinking buddies. "I'll be in touch, Ted!" he quipped, and was out the door.

Thelonious reached up to rub his shoulder, the pads on his paw meeting a stickiness where Sidebottom's hand had been. He gave his paw a discreet sniff. He might not be Winnie-the-Pooh, but he knew honey when he smelled it—and unless he was mistaken, this was lavender honey. Norfolk was known for its lavender fields. Fag-stain Man and the beekeeper were still engrossed in conversation at the bar. Although the inspector had shaken hands with both men, the beekeeper's hand had been the last thing he'd touched before Thelonious' shoulder.

He didn't bother re-checking the soles of his trainers, since he now knew what it was that he'd been stepping in.

Chapter Five

VINNIE CRAWLED OUT OF HIS STALE-smelling bed at half ten the next morning. He felt like death warmed over. He'd had a right case of the shits all night, and he knew from what—that poncey ready-meal he'd had for his tea the day before. Pavement pizza, that's what it was. Perfect for them poncey city boys in their poncey apartments, but not for *real* men like Vinnie Clark.

"Fuckin' hell, Vinnie! At least ya could've sprayed the bog with that air freshener!" cried Desmond, making a fast beeline out of the toilet before he'd had a chance to use it. "Ya tryin' to kill me or what?"

"Yeah, well, ya shoulda let me go down the chippy instead of feedin' me that—"

"It weren't that bad."

"Tell it to me gut," moaned Vinnie, rubbing his beer paunch as if it pained him.

Desmond shook his head. He knew better than to try to

reason with his brother.

Wearing only his Y-fronts, Vinnie clomped down the stairs and into the kitchen, where he grabbed a tin of lager from out of the fridge. He took it into the lounge, flopping down onto the sofa and clicking on the TV, channel surfing for porn. Taking a shit always put him in the mood to see some gash. Desmond soon joined him, but instead of having a fraternal wank in front of the telly, he grabbed the remote from Vinnie's hand. "Oi! Gimme that!" yelled Vinnie in outrage, his lager sloshing onto the sofa's upholstery. He wiped it away with his fingers, licking them dry.

Desmond's first thought was whether his brother had bothered to wash his hands after using the toilet. Somehow he doubted it. "We got things to discuss, Vinnie," he said.

"What, *now?*" Vinnie glared at him. "Can't ya see I'm lookin' for some action?"

Desmond was in a serious mood and his expression showed it. Of the two Clark brothers, he was the level-headed one, which usually meant he had to bail the hot-headed Vinnie out of scrapes—and Vinnie was always getting into scrapes. "We gotta plan our next job—and we can't be doin' it with *that* in our faces." Desmond gestured with his head toward a close-up shot of a hairless vagina on the screen. It was so magnified that it looked like something from out of a science-fiction film. The image went black as he clicked off the television.

Vinnie snorted. "If I had some of that in me face, I'd be happy as Larry."

"If that posh geezer from up west keeps givin' us work, you'll have so much gash you'll be chokin' on it."

"Suits me," Vinnie retorted with a lager-infused burp.

The Clarks were heading up to Norfolk again, the sight of their last job, which had given all-new meaning to the term "child's play." If it got any easier, they might as well be stealing the money instead of having it paid to them. Since getting out of the nick, they needed to keep a low profile, so it was better to work out of town. They didn't know anyone in Norfolk, which reduced the chances of their being recognised. The county was full of inbreeds and transplanted London ponces anyway—not the sort the Clarks associated with. Not that the Clarks did much "associating" other than going down the pub or the betting shop or releasing some city boy from the ownership of his Rolex.

The brothers owned a late-model white transit van that looked like all the other late-model white transit vans on the road. It was the perfect motor—park it on any street in any city or town or village and no one gave it a second look. It was also dead handy for transporting items from one location to another, if the job required it. For this service the Clarks tacked on an additional tariff, due to the risks involved (such as being stopped by the Old Bill). Disposing of the item necessitated yet another tariff, since there was always a further risk—that of eyewitnesses, who occasionally had to be disposed of, calling for still more tariffs and fees, and so on and so on. Only thing the brothers *didn't* tack on was VAT—and that was only because they weren't VAT registered.

A simple job could get pretty expensive for the punter, and the Clarks didn't do business on credit or easy-payment schemes like a high street furniture shop. It was cash only, with half paid up front, the rest on completion. To this day they'd never had anyone try to weasel out of paying the final instalment. Okay, they did get some wise guy who'd tried, but that was a one-off, and he'd changed his tune sharpish when his sprog went missing. Vinnie had been in the geezer's kitchen putting the screws into him, describing in lurid detail how Desmond was right at that moment snipping off the kid's fingers with a pair of gardening shears when in reality he was at the neighbourhood park, buying the little monster a Cornetto from the ice cream van. For weeks the brothers had pissed themselves laughing at the bloke's expression when Desmond had waltzed into the house with the lad, whose hands and mouth were smeared with melted chocolate from his ice cream that—at least from where his old man was sitting—looked like blood.

"We gotta get the van MOT-ed," said Desmond. "I ain't takin' any chances that we have a breakdown."

"So take it down the garage then," replied Vinnie with another burp. "It ain't like we can't afford it."

Desmond fiddled nervously with the TV remote, turning it every which way before finally setting it down onto the coffee table alongside Vinnie's pungent sock-covered feet. "Well, yeah, that's kinda what I been meanin' to talk to ya about."

Vinnie fixed his brother with a hard stare. He already knew where this was going. It was the same conversation every fucking time they did a job. It was the conversation they'd had before they'd ended up in the nick, too, and, though he didn't want to admit it, Desmond had a point.

"We gotta be careful this time," Desmond continued. "All this splashin' about—we can't risk goin' back inside, Vinnie."

"Ya think I want that?"

"No. I'm just sayin' we gotta watch our backs. No more splashin' out on birds what can't keep their big fat gobs shut."

"Ya see any birds round 'ere? Only bird I saw was that tasty bit a gash on the telly before ya got rid of it."

Desmond sighed with a heaviness he should've been used to by now. His brother was one of them geezers who always had to get some. Not that Desmond had anything against getting his leg over, but Vinnie went for them dumb slappers that were all tits and no brain. Not that Desmond had anything against tits either. Problem was, these bints went mouthing off to their mates whenever a bloke was splashing the money about. *That* was what landed them in it the last time.

"Bruv, ya worry too much," said Vinnie, chugging down the last of his lager. He propelled himself up from the sofa, returning to the kitchen to get a replacement, Desmond hot on his heels. "You're gonna grow old before your time, mate. Ya gotta do what's effectively known as 'chillin' out'!" He stuck his shaved head inside the fridge. "You'll get a heart attack if ya keep on like this."

Having Vinnie Clark as your brother was enough to give you a coronary, no doubt about it, Desmond mused sourly. Though that was the price you paid when you needed some proper muscle on a job. Not that Desmond wasn't equally capable of smashing in some geezer's skull, but Vinnie did it so well. With him it was an art. Problem was, Vinnie enjoyed his art just a bit too much. His temper had forced Desmond to walk on eggshells ever since they were lads; you never knew when something would set him off. No surprise he'd earned the nickname "Psycho Vinnie" over the years. Despite the high crime rate in their East London neighbourhood, they'd never once had their house burgled or their van mucked about with. Not even the local gangs dared to mess with the Clarks. Desmond knew he was fooling himself if he didn't admit it was all down to his brother.

Unfortunately, Vinnie was a loose cannon—and Desmond didn't plan to stick around when it went off for the last time. If things continued as they had been, he'd have enough squirreled away to get out of Bow and away from his brother and everything else in this shithole called London. His plan was to get a place on the beach in the Costa Brava and lie about drinking Spanish sangria all day and shagging fit Spanish birds all night. All he needed was to get through these next couple of jobs with Vinnie.

Desmond just hoped his psycho brother didn't get wind of his master plan or there'd be some serious hell to pay.

Chapter Six

THELONIOUS SPENT THE NEXT SEVERAL days driving about taking photographs and dodging Mrs. Baxter, keeping his evenings reserved for The Drowned Duck. DCI Sidebottom seemed to have taken leave from Little Acre's bustling social scene, though the other members were all present and accounted for: Fag-stain Man holding court at the bar with his beekeeping sidekick, the Belgians and their belching Russian huddled at their table, the vicar and his wife ignoring each other and drinking like fish, and Lord Nelson romancing any chair leg that would have him. Every time the door opened, Thelonious's gut went into a clench-lock as he expected his nemesis to walk in, but it kept ending up being a false alarm, resulting in Zimmer-frame Granny or some other soul with nothing better to do than spend the evening at The Drowned Duck.

After three nights with still no sign of the inspector, Thelonious wondered if something had happened to him.

Though surely in a village of this size, if anything untoward *had* taken place (such as Sidebottom being shot and killed by a drug-crazed gun-wielding sheep rustler), it would've been the talk of the pub. Therefore Thelonious amused himself with the more pedestrian fate of Mrs. Sidebottom's Cottage Pie landing her husband in hospital with food poisoning. With any luck, it would prove fatal.

On a weekday morning after one of Mrs. Baxter's tinned and processed breakfasts, Thelonious decided to drive to nearby Kelton Market to fuel up the Mini. He'd finally managed to pick up a replacement stepladder and it was now safely ensconced in the boot of the car, waiting to be put into use. According to the SATNAV, there was a petrol station located at the edge of the village on the road he'd be approaching from. Kelton Market was famous for its popular street market. The fact that it also happened to be the scene of a recent murder gave it a rather *noir* appeal that Thelonious had mixed feelings about. But the village was one of Norfolk's most popular attractions. It would be remiss of him not to at least investigate its photographic potential.

For Thelonious the business of buying petrol was an exercise in misery and humiliation. Despite having a stepladder on hand for these kinds of tasks, it was still something he'd have given anything to avoid. Alas, customer service appeared to be a thing of the past, especially when it came to petrol stations. It only existed in those old American films—the ones that showed some teenaged lad with a big cheesy grin filling a customer's car with petrol as if it were the biggest honour of his life. Thelonious pined for a world such as this where everyone went out of his or her way to be helpful and pleasant and wasn't out to pick your pocket at every turn. It was one of the reasons he'd been so excited about coming to Norfolk—to find a bit of the past.

So far it seemed to be eluding him.

Kelton Market's one and only petrol station, which also functioned as an automotive repair shop, was right where the SATNAV said it would be, its tiny forecourt cluttered with cars either awaiting repair or having been repaired. Thelonious zigzagged the Mini around them, pulling up to the ancient fuel dispenser. For several minutes he sat drumming his paws against the steering wheel, hoping that some cheesy-grinned lad would come running out to serve him. Finally accepting the fact that it wasn't going to happen, he shut off the engine and embarked upon the task of extricating himself from the Mini—a process made more unpleasant than usual due to his bloated gut.

Thelonious had been feeling a bit windy ever since breakfast, thanks to all those tinned beans. Even while he was busy shovelling them into his mouth he had known it was a bad idea, but he'd been starving, having eaten his dinner far too early the evening before. He could thank DCI Sidebottom for that. He'd been so worried his luck wouldn't hold that he ate two hours earlier than usual to avoid running into the inspector. As if to spite him, the man didn't even show up!

As for the breakfast menu at Baxter House, it was all well and good to stick to a budget, but surely there had to be limits on how much cheap and nasty food a B&B could get away with fobbing off on their guests. Mrs. Baxter appeared to be the reigning queen of tinned food. Perhaps she bought tinned fried eggs and tinned bacon and tinned toast as well as tinned beans, since everything she served had a metallic taste to it, including her cups of tea. Although Thelonious wasn't any great shakes in the kitchen like those celebrity chefs on TV, at least he didn't make a habit of eating things that had been stored inside a metal container since the last millennium. As he experienced yet another unpleasant surge of air inflating his gut, he wondered if this was his comeuppance for his mean-spirited thoughts about DCI Sidebottom and his wife's Cottage Pie.

Not yet ready to give up on the possibility of help with the petrol, Thelonious reached inside the car to give the horn a friendly tap, hoping this might spark some action. When it didn't, he fixed his furry visage with his most ferocious glare and directed it toward the garage, as if sheer force of will would prompt someone to emerge from the automotive chaos. The only sign of life was in the form of a filthy pair of trainers sticking out from beneath the front of a black Audi that had been reversed into the garage—and whoever's feet they belonged to didn't look in any hurry to scoot out from under the chassis. Knowing when it was time to admit defeat, Thelonious slammed the car door and went to open the boot. As he leaned inside to haul out the stepladder, the turmoil in his stomach that had been threatening to erupt finally did and he took perverse pleasure in the fact that the wind direction would take the effluvium straight to the man beneath the Audi. Lord Nelson would've been proud!

Securing the ladder into place, Thelonious climbed up three quarters of the way and reached for the handle of the fuel valve, hoping it wouldn't be mucked up with grease and spilled petrol. It amazed him that so many drivers still didn't know how to properly pump petrol and ended up leaving behind an oily mess for the next customer. Removing the stink of petrol from fur was not an easy task. Nor, for that matter, was paying for it, as Thelonious soon found out when he couldn't locate any buttons on the pump that would allow him to pre-pay with a credit or debit card.

Indeed, the blasted thing was positively antique. It must've been there since the Second World War, if not the Battle of Trafalgar. Quaint was fine, if you ran a shop selling lace doilies and kitschy teacups, but it was *not* fine for a petrol station in 21st century Britain. Just as Thelonious resigned himself to having to go inside the garage to roust the mechanic who'd obviously fallen asleep beneath the Audi, he noticed a handwritten note taped to the fuel dispenser. In order to read it, he had to climb up onto the top-most portion of the ladder, where he teetered precariously.

PLEASE PAY INSIDE WHEN DONE.

Thelonious would have burst into laughter had he not been concerned he'd fall off the ladder and break his neck. Nevertheless, he felt heartened by the simple note. It indicated a sense of trust and a faith in the honesty of one's fellow man. He liked that. Maybe Norfolk *did* have what he needed.

His vantage point from the ladder allowed Thelonious an unobstructed view of the red, white and blue of the Union Jack on the Mini's roof, which now included a generous amount of black and grey-green drips and dabs executed in Jackson Pollack style, albeit with less artistry. Although he wasn't a fan of abstract art, considering it for the most part pretentious twaddle, the birds at Baxter House clearly held a different opinion as to what constituted art. Thelonious suspected the gang of crows that were always hanging about the B&B's car park like a bunch of hoodies up to no good. From now on he'd make a point to park farther away from the tree, since that seemed to be the equivalent of their local pub. In the meantime, he needed to find a car wash, since he wasn't about to drive all over Norfolk with a desecration of his country's flag on top of his car.

It was his typical dumb luck that the moment he'd finished filling the tank and packing the ladder back into the boot was the moment the owner of the filthy trainers decided to crawl out from beneath the vehicle he'd been working on to collect payment. Not that Thelonious was planning to drive off without paying, but a less honest individual could have got away with it quite easily. "Everything all right?" asked the mechanic/attendant, stuffing the bank notes Thelonious gave him into the grease-stained pocket of his coveralls.

Thelonious wanted to say no, it was *not* all right and what he'd really needed was some service, but he knew he'd be wasting his breath. The fellow looked as dumb as a post. He pitied the owner of the black Audi, if Einstein here was the one in charge of repairing it.

Or at least Thelonious pitied the Audi's owner until he saw the residential parking permit stuck to the vehicle's windscreen. What were the odds of there being more than one late-model black Audi with a parking permit from the same London borough in this part of Norfolk? Resisting the urge to take his key to the vehicle's expensive paint job, he continued on his way.

Rather than having a quick look around as he'd originally intended, Thelonious decided to spend the day in Kelton Market and see what he could shoot (other than the Audi's owner if he ever came bumper-to-bumper with him again). He found a parking space at the bottom of the high street and figured he'd better grab it rather than risk losing it on the off chance he might find one in the centre of the village. Granted, he'd need to walk a lot farther, but at least he wouldn't have to come to blows over it. Although Kelton Market was best known for its arts and antiques market, it only operated on weekends. But if he found enough photographic potential, he'd return on market day. It might be worthwhile capturing some images of people going about their business with the traders. He'd make sure to bring along some release forms, just in case.

Thelonious's appearance in the village elicited the usual stares and snickers which, despite a lifelong struggle to remain immune to them, still managed to sting. Although he could excuse children for not having enough sense to avoid gawping, adults were a different matter, and he did his best to ignore them, ambling along the narrow pavement hoping he wouldn't get mowed down by pedestrians or a random bicyclist.

Kelton Market seemed busy for a weekday, though that was probably attributable to the start of the summer tourist season, which was further aided by the beautiful weather. Like most of his fellow Brits, Thelonious enjoyed warm sunny days—maybe because they were more rare than the gloomy ones—and he found himself feeling quite chirpy as he made his way toward the heart of the village. He was finding it difficult to see, however, as he became progressively dwarfed by those around him. Not that this was unusual, but it was as if he'd suddenly found himself walking among human skyscrapers. Were the people in this country getting taller? Though admittedly, *everyone* was tall to Thelonious, he'd been noticing a lot more six-foot-plus-ers around, especially of the male variety. If this was indicative of a physiological trend in the human species, pretty soon ladders would become obsolete!

Although his lack of stature had never made him feel inadequate, it was the reactions of others, not to mention the daily inconveniences he suffered, that made life seem like more bother than it should be. Yet Thelonious always managed to keep his spirits from sinking too low. In many ways he felt blessed—he had a special talent he could earn a living from and he was content with his own company. Things could have been worse. Many of his kind never ventured out in public, preferring to live rough and well away from the eyes and ears of human society. The ones who didn't kept mostly to themselves, living an almost monastic existence that allowed them to avoid engaging with others unless it was absolutely necessary. Among these individuals was the occasional entrepreneurial spirit like himself who'd discovered a way to earn a living in human society without actually having to join their rat race.

For those whose skills leaned more toward brawn than brain, they gravitated toward such places as building sites, where their physical strength was considered a commodity. Although it was an honest living, Thelonious got depressed every time he saw his ursine brothers crowded into a bus or underground train at rush hour, their once-lush fur dusty with rubble and encrusted with mortar. These were not the more diminutive creatures like himself, but rather those of the large and intimidating sort that would've been more at home in the rugged mountains of Banff than crammed in with a bunch of stale commuters on a bus or tube train that smelled of wet dog. Many had been brought into the country to take up the slack when the Polish builders began their exodus back home to Poland, Britain and its faltering economy having outlived its usefulness. Thelonious suspected these ursine labourers were paid a lot less than their Polish counterparts, which wasn't surprising since they had no one representing their interests. The unions refused to acknowledge or accept them, and the government simply looked the other way.

As for those of his kind lacking in skills and ambition, not to mention moral character, they resorted to other means to get by, such as thievery and becoming squatters in empty houses rather than paying their way in the world. Considering their methods of survival, it didn't seem too different from living in the wild, minus the criminal bent. As for Thelonious, he'd realised early on that he liked his creature comforts. Living in a squat with a bunch of smelly scroungers or scavenging in the wild and sleeping away an entire season was not the life for him. Besides, how would he survive without his beloved Charlie Parker?

Thelonious began to experience a sense of déjà vu as he progressed along the high street. There was a familiarity to the shop fronts and the people he saw going in and coming out of them, yet he'd never in his life been here. And the closer he got to the main centre of the village, the stronger the feeling became. Then it dawned on him—Kelton Market reminded him of Hunter's Cove, where he'd eaten that ridiculous burger in that ridiculous gastropub owned by that ridiculous ginger-haired celebrity chef.

Trendy boutiques and art galleries populated both sides of the high street, spreading out in each direction until the business district ended and the road became residential. Thelonious didn't see a single shop that offered every-day goods to the locals—unless the locals' every-day goods consisted of expensive designer clothing and overpriced paintings of Norfolk seascapes and wheat fields. The only business that provided anything of a more practical nature was a pub—and its facade had been cordoned off by a ribbon of yellow police tape. The painting of a black stag on the sign above the front entrance told Thelonious where he was.

The pub held an air of abandonment, despite having been open for business just a few days ago. Although Thelonious didn't believe in ghosts, he felt an eerie shiver move down his spine and was relieved to be standing in the sunshine across the road from The Black Stag rather than in the shadows in front of it. He looked away out of respect for the dead and for the sense of mourning he felt emanating from the place. It saddened him that even a small village in rural Norfolk had been affected by the taint of the world.

As he turned to continue on his way, Thelonious heard a familiar voice calling out to him. His gut went into a clench-lock. He ducked behind a young woman pushing a pram, but there was no avoiding the inevitable. His luck had finally run out.

"Ted!" DCI Horatio Sidebottom's voice rang out with its usual false jocularity, carrying loudly across the road and putting Thelonious instantly on his guard. The inspector was standing at the entrance to The Black Stag where, a moment earlier, there had been nothing but shadows. As he set about squeezing his clumsy bulk beneath the police tape, Thelonious could almost hear the squealing protest of unused muscles; the man wouldn't be making a career change to limbo dancer any time soon. He watched in dismay as his nemesis hurried across the high street toward him, his progress provoking a few annoyed blasts of the horn from vehicles as he dodged the midday traffic.

The inspector came to a breathless halt on the pavement directly in front of Thelonious, his broad brow speckled with perspiration from an exertion he clearly wasn't accustomed to. In Thelonious's opinion, the only kind of exercise the DCI looked capable of managing was that of bringing a forkful of food to his mouth. "And what brings *yew* to Kelton Market on this fine day?"

The words delivered a pong of raw onions and partially digested beef mince into Thelonious's nostrils and he winced, guessing Big Mac. He couldn't decide which was worse—the public embarrassment of being shouted to in the street or the stench of Sidebottom's lunch being worked over by stomach acids. The inspector couldn't have addressed him any louder than if he'd done so with a bullhorn. A number of people turned to stare, in addition to those who'd stopped dead in their tracks. Had there been a large rock in the vicinity, Thelonious would've crawled beneath it and remained there for the next few winters.

"Pub's shut if yew were of a mind for a quick pint," said Sidebottom, his tongue working to clear something away from his back teeth. Thelonious envisioned a partially chewed onion along with a bit of pickle stuck behind the inspector's molars and nearly brought up the remains of Mrs. Baxter's tinned breakfast.

Pulling down his deerstalker hat to more effectively cover his ears, Thelonious squared his shoulders, hoping to at least retain the illusion of dignity if nothing else. "Too early in the day for me," he replied, not bothering to disguise the accompanying growl from his throat.

Sidebottom exploded with laughter, his farmer's face turning the florid pink of someone suffering from high blood pressure. He reminded Thelonious of a balloon that had a face drawn onto it with a felt-tip marker. If only he'd had a pin! The DCI finally stopped guffawing long enough to speak. "Funny, but I never took *yew* for a teetotaller, Ted."

Again with the *Ted* business. Thelonious felt his claws lengthening as his ursine bloodlust threatened to take over. If the inspector carried on like this, he'd have another murder on his hands—his own. He wondered if he should try to make a run for it rather than digging himself into an even deeper hole than he already seemed to be in, what with the amount of attention he'd garnered from this emissary from Norfolk CID. Then again, it wasn't as though Sidebottom couldn't track him down. Aside from knowing where Thelonious was staying, there probably weren't many photojournalist bears in the area or, for that matter, in the country. In fact, Thelonious knew of none…*anywhere*. Had his gut not calmed down from Mrs. Baxter's beans, he would've given the inspector an olfactory treat he'd never forget. Then they would see who'd do the running!

"That's where Pickles popped his clogs." Sidebottom

indicated with a toss of his head the cordoned-off pub across the road.

Although Thelonious hadn't been acquainted with the murder victim, he took offence at the inspector's comment, which sounded flippant and lacking in empathy, particularly from someone in a position of authority. But then, what did he know? The closest he'd ever come to the inner workings of a police detective was from watching TV crime dramas. Once again Lieutenant Columbo sprang to mind—all DCI Sidebottom needed was a rumpled raincoat and a smelly old dog to make the image complete. Perhaps the publican at The Drowned Duck might loan him Lord Nelson.

Despite Thelonious's disinclination toward conversation, Sidebottom enjoyed the sound of his own voice enough to keep it going. "Shopping for souvenirs? Bit pricey round here, if yew don't mind me saying. Things are sure changing in this county—and not for the better. Lots of changes since I was a lad. Lots of changes…"

Fearing the inspector was about to revisit memory lane by regaling him with fond tales of when he was still wearing short trousers, Thelonious fixed his furry visage in his best attempt at a scowl, hoping this might discourage any reminiscences. He felt like asking the DCI if he didn't have some actual police work to crack on with, but thought better of it.

As if reading his thoughts, Sidebottom's expression shifted from jovial to grim. "We don't get murders round these parts," he said, giving Thelonious a hard stare full of suspicion.

If the rewind button of this refrain was pushed one more time, Thelonious wouldn't be held accountable for his actions. His teeth gnashed together and he suppressed the urge to fasten them onto the inspector's leg. The DCI seemed determined to find guilt where none existed and he wondered how many members of Norfolk's population falsely confessed to crimes they hadn't committed just to get shot of this character.

"Derrick Pickles was a good man," continued Sidebottom, actually sounding tearful. "To be cut down in the prime of life like that, it's not right…not right at all."

To his surprise, Thelonious found himself nodding in agreement. The inspector was right—it *was* a dreadful thing to have happened. Perhaps it would be better to live in the wild instead of in this place they called "civilisation." At least then he'd be among his own kind, leading a simpler existence. Life among humans wasn't all it was cracked up to be. However, there *were* those creature comforts….

Sidebottom shook his head, making appropriate noises of dismay. Despite his distress over poor Derrick Pickles being so unfairly taken in the prime of his life, he didn't appear to be in any big hurry to return to the business of solving his murder. Thelonious made a show of checking his wristwatch, then cast an exaggerated look over his shoulder at the shop behind him—a bespoke clothier for men, waiting for the inspector to take the hint and realise he had other things to do than stand about chewing the fat all day. Not that Thelonious intended to conduct any business in this particular shop, but what DCI Sidebottom didn't know wouldn't hurt him.

The minutes ticked past until the inspector finally caught on. "I see I'm keeping yew from your shopping," he said with a sigh of disappointment, his eyes taking in the exclusive-looking clothiers. "I'd best be off then." Without another word, he crossed back over to the other side of the high street, manoeuvring his bulk beneath the police tape with all the grace of a baby elephant. He stood in the doorway of the pub, observing Thelonious with fresh suspicion.

Thelonious wanted to cross the road himself so that he could draw some cash out of the hole in the wall at the bank. However, the inspector's scrutiny had got him so rattled that he didn't pay as much attention to safety as he should have. Just as he stepped from the kerb, a black Audi came flying toward him at a speed well in excess of the legal limit for a built-up area, its front tyre nearly clipping his foot as it passed. Although it all happened very quickly, Thelonious still had time to see the London parking permit on the vehicle's windscreen.

As he raised his arm to shake his paw at the driver and let out a threatening roar, he suddenly remembered that he had an audience. DCI Sidebottom continued to loiter in The Black Stag's doorway, his attention riveted to Thelonious, who reversed a few steps, ending up right back in the same place he'd been when the inspector had first ambushed him—and consequently directly in front of the bespoke clothiers. It seemed he had no choice but to go into the shop, especially since he'd given the inspector the impression it was his intended destination. Maybe if he dallied inside long enough, Sidebottom would grow bored and go off to conduct some police business, leaving Thelonious to get on with *his* business.

Since finding clothes that fit him was a never-ending challenge, he reckoned it couldn't hurt to take a quick look at what was on offer, even if he probably couldn't afford any of it. Just the word "bespoke" conjured up images of expensively tailored suits worn by perfectly groomed men who looked as if they'd stepped out of the pages of *GQ* magazine. Where would Thelonious even wear such a thing? Although it was always possible one of his photographs might win an award—at least then he'd have something to look smart in at the awards ceremony!

Not surprisingly, Thelonious couldn't reach the door handle and was forced to rap against the glass until someone finally took notice of him waiting outside. Several moments dragged past before the door was grudgingly opened by a man with a nose that could've been stuck into a pencil sharpener, it was that long and thin. He was dressed in a suit that made Thelonious's wallet feel lighter already. Though he didn't much care for the look of the fellow, he had to admit that was one spiffy suit he was wearing. If this was an example of their wares, the financial outlay might be worth considering.

Thelonious trundled past him into the shop, nearly butting his head on the corner of a table set too close to the door. A number of fabric samples had been arranged upon its polished wood surface in neat overlapping rows, including some nice summer-weight tweeds. Dressmaker dummies were placed strategically around the shop's interior, some displaying jackets, others tailored shirts—none of which Thelonious could envision himself wearing, but maybe it *was* time to spruce up his act. Although "bespoke" conjured up overpriced in his mind, a shop in Norfolk should still be a damned sight cheaper than anything in London—or at least that was what he thought until he caught sight of the price list.

This was well out of his league. Though surely those prices were for the adult-sized human male whose clothing required far more in the way of fabric and labour rather than the more diminutive customer such as himself? Perhaps in his case the prices could be halved. Considering his size, they really should be cut to a quarter, but Thelonious thought that would be pushing it.

A quick glance through the glass-fronted door indicated that DCI Sidebottom hadn't budged from his sentry duty outside The Black Stag. It appeared Thelonious would need to hang about for a while longer until the coast was clear. Fixing his furry visage into an expression worthy of the most hard-core of clothes shoppers, he proceeded to check out the displays, expecting the snooty-looking salesman to ask if he required assistance. Instead the fellow went to sit behind a small antique desk, where he examined some invoices, the contents of which must've been infinitely fascinating, judging from the intense concentration being given to them. Clearly he didn't work on commission.

Thelonious cleared his throat, at last attracting the salesman's attention, though that still wasn't sufficient to prompt him to come out from behind the desk. On the contrary, he gave Thelonious an exasperated stare, as if he'd just discovered a smudge of dirt on his trouser leg. "Would these prices be less for someone of my stature?" Thelonious was embarrassed to have to ask the question, but he didn't like wasting money. Besides, it seemed perfectly logical to him that they would be less.

However, it did not seem perfectly logical to the salesman, who thrust his pencil nose high in the air, his countenance souring as if he'd been grievously insulted. "Those, *sir*, are our prices. I'm afraid they are *not* open to negotiation."

Once again the urge to bite took hold of Thelonious, and it was all he could do to stop himself from attaching his jaw to the salesman's leg and ripping out a chunk of flesh. Maybe if the pencil-nosed git had a bit of leg missing, he too might feel that he warranted a discounted price on his next bespoke suit. Rather than getting into an altercation—especially with DCI Sidebottom lurking across the road—Thelonious let it go. Having had enough of being treated like a second-class citizen by the shop's hired help, he trundled to the door, where he was for the second time thwarted by the inaccessibility of the handle. So much for a dignified exit, he mused in frustration. He cleared his throat several times, the last emerging as a full-on roar, which finally motivated the salesman to leave the sanctity of his desk. With a smarmy smile, he pulled open the door, moving out of the way to allow Thelonious through. "Have a good afternoon, *sir*."

Thelonious stepped outside onto the pavement, relieved to be back in the wholesome Norfolk sunshine and fresh air. The shop door slammed shut behind him. Had he been standing a couple of centimetres closer, it would've whacked him on his backside. His eyes anxiously sought out The Black Stag; DCI Sidebottom had abandoned his watch and was nowhere in sight. If nothing else had been accomplished at the clothiers, at least his delaying tactics had been successful. Unfortunately, his creative mood was ruined. The last thing Thelonious felt like doing was taking photos in the village. He'd have to leave it for market day. Not that he had much faith in capturing anything authentically Norfolk, if what he'd seen and experienced of the famous Kelton Market was an indication of things to come.

He clomped down the high street toward where he'd left the Mini, darting between pedestrians and nearly tripping them up in his haste to put as much distance between himself and DCI Sidebottom as possible. Thelonious just wanted to draw a line through this complete waste of a morning. Maybe once he got away from here, his mood might change and he'd feel up to getting his camera out again. On reaching the car, his heart sank. A host of fresh bird droppings speckled the bonnet and windscreen, along with some added contributions on the already desecrated Union Jack. Decision made. Before he did anything else today, he'd visit the car wash, because no way in hell was he driving around in a vehicle splattered with bird shit. It simply wasn't dignified!

Fortunately Thelonious remembered having driven through a decent-sized town not far from Little Acre where he'd seen one of those drive-thru car washes. Since there were also some sites of historical interest nearby, it made sense to head out that way and try to salvage what remained of his work day. He'd get the Mini sorted first, after which he'd check out the sites, take some photos, then reward himself with a pint and an early dinner at a pub in the area. He thought he'd give The Drowned Duck a miss tonight. The way things were going, DCI Sidebottom was bound to turn up—and one dose per day of the inspector was enough. In fact, it was one dose too many.

Programming the SATNAV for his next port of call, Thelonious drove a short distance down the road until he could safely turn around, then headed back up the high street and into the centre of the village as the computerised female voice instructed. Just as he came parallel to the bespoke clothiers, the door opened. The pencil-nosed salesman stepped outside and began to light up a fag. Unable to resist, Thelonious stuck his paw out the driver's-side window and shook it menacingly—or as menacingly as possible considering that the gesture was being made by a diminutively statured bear driving a Mini Cooper with a shit-spattered Union Jack on the roof. The fellow's thin lips shaped themselves into an astonished O, his face reddening. For good measure, Thelonious let loose with his best ursine roar, its impact somewhat diminished by Charlie Parker's sax.

Feeling satisfied with himself, he checked the rear-view mirror as he passed, noting that the salesman hadn't moved from his spot on the pavement. He was no longer alone, however. He'd been joined by DCI Sidebottom, who must've gone inside the clothiers at some point after Thelonious had left. Despite the image growing smaller with distance, he could still make out the look of suspicion on the inspector's face. If the DCI *had* been inside the shop, Thelonious doubted if it was to get measured up for a new suit.

After a series of wrong turns that set his jangled nerves further on edge, Thelonious eventually reached Barnham—a town that boasted a high street featuring all the usual frozen-food emporiums, discount pound shops, betting dens, greeting card shops, estate agents, charity shops, banks and building societies. Fed up with being told to turn where he should *not* be turning, he switched off the SATNAV and tried to remember where he'd seen the car wash, certain it was located by a supermarket. Considering his day so far, Thelonious didn't expect to find it without a fight; therefore he was pleasantly surprised when his luck decided to change and he came to a sign indicating a supermarket. He veered off in the direction specified, hoping there wasn't more than one. About a quarter of a mile later he saw the hulking mass of a supermarket on the right and—along with it—the car wash.

"*Hasta la vista*, bird shit!" he roared, making a bee-line into the empty forecourt. Thelonious had imagined the place would be busy, what with it still being the lunch hour, but his was the only car there. At least he wouldn't have to waste yet more valuable time, he thought as he extricated himself from the Mini to go inside to pay. Perhaps the day wouldn't be a complete loss, after all.

Unfortunately the girl at the till seemed far more

interested in the miniature TV set featuring a cat fight between council-estate chavs on *The Jeremy Kyle Show* than serving customers—and no amount of throat clearing on Thelonious's part could compete with the din of shouting and swearing coming from these high priestesses of Estuary English. The cashier's choice of attire—a shiny pink tracksuit accessorised with the requisite oversized gold hoop earrings—led him to conclude that she took her fashion tips from Jeremy's esteemed guests.

Thelonious finally had to resort to rattling the display rack of sweets to attract the girl's attention, in the process knocking several packets of Maynards wine gums to the floor, which he didn't bother to pick up. At long last she dragged her eyes away from the televised bloodshed, only to gawp at Thelonious as if she'd never seen anyone of his ilk before, especially at a car wash. Whether she had or had not was beside the point. He was a paying customer—and there was no excuse for rudeness. Had there been another car wash in the vicinity, Thelonious would've taken his business there instead. What gave these people the right to look down their noses at him? He was a respected photojournalist with a publishing contract, not some chav of a cashier or pencil-nosed poof who made a living from measuring men's inside legs!

The girl came shambling out from behind the till to sullenly collect Thelonious's money. Her shiny pink tracksuit burned his eyes now that he could see it in its full chavvy glory. It took her an eternity to make change for his ten-pound note—and even after all this high finance was completed she still managed to short-change him by a pound. Although Thelonious hated being cheated, he just couldn't be bothered anymore. He'd reached the point where he felt like calling it a day. The nerves in his neck and shoulders were all bunched up, which always happened when he got stressed out. What he needed was a long soak in a hot bath. He hoped Baxter House hadn't taken in any new guests that would be competing with him for the hot water. So far he seemed to be the only one staying there—or at least as far as he could tell.

Thelonious stormed out of the shop and climbed back into the Mini, relieved that it would soon be clean of bird muck, even if it *had* cost him an extra quid. He pulled up to the entrance of the car wash, navigated the tyres onto the conveyor, and sat back to let the process begin. His stomach rumbled with hunger, competing with the ruckus taking place inside the tunnel. He really needed to keep to some kind of schedule; it wasn't healthy for him to have such long gaps between meals. As soon as he was done here, he'd find a pub, though he wouldn't do so in Barnham. The pubs he'd seen in the town centre looked like the sort that served those processed frozen meals, if the number of signs boasting the cheap and nasty specials were anything to go by. He was unlikely to find anything remotely resembling samphire on offer, let alone anything fresh. Norfolk wasn't short on villages or countryside—he'd drive around until he found somewhere that *didn't* serve food that came out of a plastic microwavable tray.

Giant brushes whizzed and whirred around the Mini, turning it into one big soap sud, lulling Thelonious into a sense of calm that was very much needed after the day he'd had thus far—a sense of calm that abruptly ended when he heard an ominous metallic clank. The car jerked to a halt, though the brushes continued to whip up an enthusiastic froth. He couldn't see a thing out of the front or rear windscreen or any of the side windows. It was as if the Mini, along with Thelonious, had been dropped into a vat of whipped cream. He waited for the conveyor to start up again and the water jets to come on, but nothing happened. It appeared he was being soaped to death.

At least ten minutes went by, though maybe it only felt like ten minutes because he was so hungry. To keep himself occupied and stave off an attack of claustrophobia, Thelonious began counting off the seconds, the plan being that if nothing happened by the time he reached one hundred, he'd begin sounding the horn to attract someone's attention. Not that he could imagine the track-suited cashier coming to his rescue, but she was the best he could hope for at the moment. Getting out of the car was not an option—the brushes had him hemmed in. He'd be lucky to get the drivers-side door open wide enough to poke out a paw, and he wasn't about to risk a frothy waterfall flooding the vehicle's interior.

Thelonious reached one hundred faster than he'd expected. The conveyor beneath the Mini's tyres still hadn't shifted into action. As the brushes continued their soapy work, he began to fear they'd remove the paint as well as the bird droppings. Could be the reason why the car wash had no customers in the middle of what should've been the lunchtime rush was because the locals already knew the place was bad news and stayed well clear of it. He sounded the horn a few times and waited. When nothing happened, he counted to one hundred a second time and waited. Still nothing happened. This time he leaned on the horn, holding it down for so long he thought he'd run down the battery. If there was no one else in the vicinity to rescue him but that dozy chav of a cashier, he'd probably die in here. He wished he'd taken the time to make a will. Not that he had a lot to leave behind, but whatever he did have he would've liked to see go to the WSPA.

Suddenly Thelonious felt a sharp jolt as the conveyor kicked back into action. The soap brushes stopped and pulled away, returning to their original dormant positions as the car was moved into the next section of tunnel, which he knew should be the rinse and dry cycles. Instead the Mini arrived at the exit in a fluffy halo of foam—and with a broken passenger-side wing mirror. Thelonious had been so rattled from dealing with the cashier that he'd forgotten to fold it in as he'd done with the one on the drivers' side.

Grateful to escape with his life, he didn't go back for the rinse cycle.

Chapter Seven

VINNIE LOVED HIS JOB. HELL, HE LIVED for it. He ate, slept and shit for it. He felt like the luckiest man alive. Just knowing he had a big job planned—the kind that involved some real hands-on labour—gave him a stonker to end all stonkers. Pity any bird that crossed his tracks when that happened. She wouldn't be able to sit or walk for a month!

He considered his work an art. There was nothing he enjoyed more than the feel of his boot stomping in some geezer's skull. That melodic crunch—it was a rush better than any hit of some poncey designer drug. These were moments to be savoured, tasted. Not even shagging a really fit bird could compare. He reckoned he probably had some Kray blood running through his veins. Sure, plenty of people from the East End laid claim to the Kray legacy, but that was mostly bollocks, a sad attempt to make them look tough and important. Vinnie didn't need to go telling tales about where he'd come from or what he was. He *knew*.

What set him aside from the rest—even from his own brother—was his approach. You couldn't do this kind of work by putting half a heart into it. There had to be a real love of the craft, a special talent. That one-eared Vincent Van Whatsit geezer didn't paint his paintings with half a heart. No. He'd been into it with every drop of blood and every gob of spit. Not that Vinnie knew sweet fuck all about art, but there you have it. You had to have a good work ethic too, which he did—not like some of them lazy gits he'd been banged up with. They did things the sloppy way, leaving a lot of loose ends. Well, not Vinnie Clark. Loose ends could get you killed or, at the very least, get you banged up again. And he wasn't about to let the Old Bill get their stinking hands on him a second time! As for Desmond, though Vinnie felt a strong sense of fraternal responsibility for him, he worried his brother didn't have enough bottle. He couldn't risk being dragged down. He'd need to keep a closer watch on Desmond to stop that from happening.

Pride. That was the key. A geezer couldn't be successful if he didn't take pride in what he did. That was the problem with this country—nobody took pride in their work anymore. Vinnie blamed the foreigners. How could anyone British feel a sense of pride when the entire country was swarming with moochers and freeloaders from every third-world shithole? These days you couldn't even find a brothel that wasn't being run by some fucking Albanian or Russian. Not that Vinnie went to brothels. He'd never had trouble pulling birds—and he didn't mean mingers either, so he didn't need to pay for it. But he knew plenty of geezers who'd lost their trade when that vodka-swilling filth had moved in. An Englishman couldn't be an entrepreneur in his own country these days. It was shameful.

Well, he'd be damned if he let these foreign scum ruin it for him. No one was taking a piss on the Clark brothers!

Vinnie loitered in the pub's dimly lighted kitchen, stuffing chips into his mouth that had been left behind in the chip pan from when the publican had shut for the night. They'd gone cold and were as greasy as the engine in their transit van, but killing always gave him an appetite. Desmond gaped at him from the door leading to the alleyway, his latex-covered hand clutching the handle even though their work wasn't done. "Vinnie, what the fuck ya doin'?" he cried. "We gotta finish up and get out of 'ere, not be muckin' about with a midnight snack."

"Problem with you, bruv," replied Vinnie through a mouthful of chips, "ya worry too much. Ya gotta chill."

"*Chill?* We got a dead geezer lyin' on the floor! And his blood's all over the effin' place!"

Frowning, Vinnie turned up the rubber soles of his Doc Martens to inspect for damage, wiping them clean on the dead man's clothing, after which he finished off what remained of the chips. "Could sure do with a pint," he said, licking the grease from his latex-gloved fingertips. The fact that they'd just held the tyre iron that had bashed in a man's skull didn't faze him. He grasped the tyre iron in his other hand as if he might need to use it again, dripping blood onto the worn lino. "Worked up a right thirst tonight. Hope he's got some decent lager."

"What, ya mean *here*?"

"Sure, why not? It's a pub, innit?"

"Yeah, Vinnie, it's a pub. Ya want maybe I should switch on all the lights out front and tell the locals we're open for business? We'll say that ol' Ollie 'ere," Desmond nudged the corpse with the steel toe of his boot, "just needed a little lie-down. How's that?"

"Ya really take all the fun outta life."

Desmond shook his balaclava-covered head that was identical to his brother's balaclava-covered head right down to the shaved surfaces beneath. If Vinnie had his way, they'd be having a post-killing party in the bar, complete with strippers and DJ. Why his brother always felt the need to hang about after offing someone Desmond couldn't imagine. Guess he got some kind of sick thrill from it.

"'Ere, gimme that!" Grabbing the tyre iron from Vinnie,

Desmond wiped the gore from it on the dead man's bloodied clothing and sighed, feeling very old all of a sudden. Hell, maybe he *was* old—or at least too old for this kind of shit. "Let's just empty the till and be done with it," he said, trying to keep the edge from his voice. It wouldn't do to go pissing off his brother, not when they had a dead body on the floor. Whenever Vinnie got like this, there was no telling him anything. It was like he'd turned into some kind of Superman and nothing could touch him. You just had to go along for the ride and hope your luck would hold. Well, Desmond knew that luck didn't last forever, not when you had Vinnie Clark for a brother. It was time to start looking after *numero uno*.

Although he wasn't happy about the situation, so far it seemed to be going okay and without any cock-ups. That posh toff from Chelsea had said to off the geezers and make it look like robbery, so that's what they did. They'd been given advance details about such things as alarm systems, CCTV cameras, and the nightly closing-up routines of staff so they wouldn't be going in blind. They reckoned everyone would blame the Gypos anyway, since they were always up to no good with their robbing and thieving and filthy ways. The Clarks wouldn't enter into the frame at all. Being East End lads, Norfolk was well out of their territory. No one would be expecting another killing, which was why they'd been told to go ahead with the second job rather than waiting for the dust to settle. By the time the coppers had it figured out, the brothers would've concluded their business in the county and be off on holiday somewhere—a holiday which, at least in Desmond's case, he planned to make permanent.

With the money from the till deposited inside a plastic Tesco bag, Vinnie and Desmond slunk out through the jimmied-open rear door of The Fat Badger where they'd first come in, finding themselves in an unpaved and poorly lighted alleyway lined with rubbish bins from the pub and the neighbouring shops. They followed it along to the left, where it passed by a row of terraced cottages, terminating at a narrow road lined with still more terraced cottages. The brothers walked single-file in the centre of the cobbled road, heading uphill to where they'd parked the transit van.

The neighbourhood was as quiet as the grave, without so much as a dog barking. Other than the occasional exterior light intended to prevent burglaries, the houses were dark, the occupants behind them likely tucked up in their beds and ignorant of the deadly goings-on that had just transpired at their local. The inadequate glow of the streetlight didn't carry more than a few feet, allowing the brothers to move without much concern of being seen. They walked in silence, their rubber soles making no sound on the old cobbles. The white of their transit van was the only thing visible up ahead in the blackness and they let out relieved breaths upon reaching it, yanking off their balaclavas, their hairless heads shiny with oily perspiration.

As Vinnie settled himself behind the steering wheel, Desmond carefully wrapped the tyre iron in an old blanket they'd stored on the floor behind the passenger seat, jamming it underneath to hide it from view. He hopped into place on the seat alongside his brother, pulling the door closed with as little noise as possible. The Clarks stripped off their soiled latex gloves, tossing them into another Tesco bag, which they planned to dispose of once they were safely out of the county.

Vinnie always did the driving on jobs, preferring to be in control should something happen, and he turned the key in the ignition. The recently tuned engine sprang to life, disrupting the silence. He quickly shifted into gear, waiting until the van had gone the few remaining feet to the top of the road and turned the corner before switching on the headlights.

"Another job well done, ay, Vinnie?" chirped Desmond with a light-heartedness he didn't feel. His brother's silence always unnerved him, since you never knew what he had going on in that psycho brain of his. To make matters worse, Vinnie always had something negative to say about

Desmond's work—and he wasn't in the mood for it. All he wanted was to get the hell out of here. He'd be shitting himself till they reached the A road, where at least there'd be some traffic and they wouldn't stand out so much. The quicker they put Norfolk behind them, the better. The grim tower blocks, cheap shop fronts and general ugliness of Bow sounded like a sanctuary right now.

"Yeah, bruv. I wouldn't mind makin' this a regular thing, if I do say so meself!" said Vinnie, sounding happy as Larry.

"Well, I can't wait till it's done and dusted and we can finally start divvyin' up the dosh."

Vinnie cut a sharp glance at his brother before returning his attention to the road. "Why? What's the big hurry? Ya plannin' on goin' somewhere?"

Desmond's sphincter locked up so tight he'd probably not be able to shit for a week. Why couldn't he have kept his fat gob shut? It wouldn't do to go getting his brother thinking all sorts, not when he was so close to getting what he wanted. Vinnie had eyes like a shithouse rat—Desmond would need to be real careful what he said from hereon in. He couldn't risk him knowing about his future plans in the Costa Brava, especially when they didn't include him. Psycho Vinnie might've been his brother and his only real family, but Desmond didn't want to spend the rest of his effing life with him. "No, I ain't goin' nowhere," he answered a bit too quickly.

Vinnie continued to cut his eyes at him all the way back to London. It was the longest drive of Desmond's life.

Chapter Eight

Publican Found Dead in Apparent Robbery!
—Front page headline from *The Fens Gazette*

THELONIOUS HAD FOUND A GARAGE in the area that did a fairly decent patch-up job on his broken passenger-side wing mirror. He decided it would have to do until he could book in a repair with the nearest dealership, which was up in Norwich. Although it probably needed replacing, he'd manage for the time being. It was really more an aesthetic issue; he loved his Mini Cooper, and he wasn't about to let his standards start slipping now.

It was a beautiful summer day in Norfolk with not a cloud or raindrop predicted, so he decided to drive a bit further afield to the Fens. After the fiasco of the previous day, not to mention the wash-out at the beach before that, he was determined to make up for lost time. He refused to allow himself to be defeated by bogus parking tickets or supercilious salesman or overpriced gastropubs or chavvy cashiers or blundering police inspectors with nothing better to do than harass innocent citizens going about their business. Thelonious had a job to do, and by god, he was going to do it!

The Fens had always been a place that had fascinated him and he was pleased to have an opportunity to finally be going there. He figured he should capture some quality images of the area before the land was reclaimed by the sea, especially with all this global warming everyone kept banging on about. It was strange that a region could have problems with drought, yet still end up becoming flooded with seawater. No wonder the environmentalists were up in arms. Not that Thelonious was some frothing-at-the-mouth green activist—or *any* kind of activist, for that matter. He left that sort of thing to others. He just wanted a quiet life with the least amount of grief possible.

That was the main reason he'd decided to bite the bullet and get out of London, putting anything of value into storage and offloading the rest on Craig's List. Thelonious thought he'd travel for a while, experience new places, expand his horizons. There was a whole world out there and, unlike what most Londoners believed, it didn't revolve around the capital. Maybe he might come across a reasonably priced little cottage to rent in Norfolk that he could call home—something tidy, easy to maintain, perhaps with a small garden to relax in on a warm day and do the *Sunday Times* crossword. It wasn't that Thelonious was keen on gardening (or the crosswords), but urban landscapes were just so unnatural, especially for his kind.

His ursine brothers and sisters in the wild would never have believed it if they'd seen how he'd been living—a pokey flat with no space to put anything; paper-thin walls that allowed you to hear everything your neighbours got up to; not to mention the overall décor, which consisted of wet laundry hanging on racks in the lounge or draped over radiators. It was the twenty-first century and Thelonious, along with millions of other Londoners, were living like refugees in a World War II camp—*and* paying a premium for the privilege! By London standards, he was considered lucky to even have an off-street parking space. Not that this was any guarantee he could actually park in it, since his neighbour made a habit of blocking access to it with his motorbike. Thelonious was certain the creep did it on purpose and it was all he could do to keep from jabbing a screwdriver into the bike's tyres, letting the air out and destroying them beyond repair. The fact that the evidence would inevitably point to him as the culprit was the only thing that stopped him. Thank goodness all that nonsense was behind him now.

With deerstalker firmly in place, Thelonious relaxed behind the Mini's steering wheel, taking deep draughts of the fresh country air blowing in through the open windows. Today things were going to go *his* way. For once the weather report had been accurate—it couldn't have been a more perfect day. His spirits were soaring, along with the notes from Charlie Parker's sax, which provided the background music for the fields of wheat and giant rolls of hay that made up the landscape. It took less time than he'd expected before this golden tapestry became woven through with tiny blue ribbons framed with green. Thelonious had reached the Fens.

Leaving the main road behind, he veered off toward his first destination of the day: Wickham Marsh. The village was located on a gentle hill overlooking a meandering waterway that was so narrow in parts it could just as easily have been a ditch. A series of cobbled streets rose upward from it. They were lined at both sides with pebble-fronted cottages that looked as if they'd been constructed from peanut brittle glazed with a thick layer of honey. The cottages made Thelonious's mouth water and he wished he'd brought along some sweets to tide him over till lunch. It was like being in the middle of a children's fantasy story, and he nearly pinched himself to make certain he wasn't dreaming.

Wickham Marsh was larger than Little Acre, but not so large as to lose its quaint village flavour. Thelonious was eager to get out of the car and start taking photos. If he could capture with the camera lens even a small portion of what he perceived with the naked eye, he'd have some winning photos for his publisher. He decided to leave the Mini Cooper in a pay-and-display car park down by the fen, which would allow him as many hours as he needed. There were a number of cars parked there already, but he didn't see much of anyone about—which suited him just fine, since he needed to use his stepladder to reach the pay-and-display dispenser and preferred to do so without an audience. As he fed some pound coins into the machine, Thelonious noticed a sign advertising boat rides. Though considering there was more mud than liquid in the waterway, the tide was already on its way out to join the sea.

A handful of small boats were stuck fast in the mire—and they didn't hold much promise of going anywhere for the remainder of the day. Bad timing on Thelonious's part. Had he awakened earlier, he might've made it in time for the morning sail, but he'd never been one for all this catching of worms nonsense. Anything before nine was an affront to his physical well-being, and in winter nothing short of an earthquake would get him to stir before eleven. And England didn't get many earthquakes.

The hill leading up into the village proper wasn't steep, but between Thelonious' short legs and the weight of his camera bag slung over one shoulder it still proved a challenge. He'd been under the impression that the Fens were flat, along with the rest of the county. Clearly someone in the Norfolk tourism office was guilty of misinformation, because flat it most definitely was not. Well, at least he'd get into shape during his stay, though he didn't hold out much hope for his waistline. He was working up a hearty appetite just from having seen those peanut-brittle cottages; he'd be lucky to last another couple of hours before a pint and a tasty pub lunch would be in order. Thelonious had a really good feeling about Wickham Marsh. In fact, he had such a good feeling that he could picture himself living here. Maybe after he'd got some work done and eaten lunch he would pop into an estate agent's to see if any cottages were on offer. Not that he could afford to buy one, but renting was another matter.

Thelonious toddled determinedly up and down the narrow residential streets, trying not to lose his footing on the lumpy cobbles as he aimed his camera lens at anything he found of interest. Each cottage boasted a cheerful display of flowers in window boxes, hanging baskets, or planted in tiny side gardens, and it was all he could do not to take a nibble of the brightly coloured petals. He felt happier than he had in ages and he might have burst into song had he not wanted to draw attention to himself. When Thelonious saw a "To Let" sign from the local office of an estate agent's in front of one of the cottages, he couldn't believe his luck. Destiny had brought him to Wickham Marsh!

His diminutive stature combined with the frequent absence of pedestrian accommodation in the form of a pavement made the business of photography more hazardous than Thelonious had anticipated, and he had to keep an eye out for his personal safety as well as for any images he wished to capture with the camera. Although this shouldn't have been a concern in what he'd assumed would be a quiet residential area, he was surprised by the amount of vehicular traffic coming through. The roads were technically two-way, but there was barely room for a small car, let alone the beefy SUVs that kept roaring past at speeds well in excess of the legal limit. Thelonious nearly dropped his camera when a Range Rover sounded its horn as he stood in the road taking a wide-angle photo of a cottage he found particularly eye-catching, and he had to leap out of the way, landing on his backside against the hard cobbles. No sooner was he back in place trying to recapture the image than a black Audi came whizzing down the hill toward him, its driver giving no indication of slowing down. Thelonious trundled out of the road to safety as the car passed him in a gust of wind that launched his deerstalker hat into flight. As he bent to retrieve it from the cobbles, he was treated to a rude blast of horn from the driver. Had he not been so distracted with rescuing his hat, Thelonious would've seen the London residential parking permit affixed to the vehicle's windscreen.

As usual, passers-by stopped to stare at Thelonious and he had to refrain from sending a threatening growl in their direction, along with a generous showing of teeth. He tried his best to ignore them, snapping off a few photos of the cottage with the "To Let" sign so that he could review them later that evening when he was back at the B&B. If the experts' predictions came true and these Fens villages along with the entire Norfolk coastline on inland got reclaimed by the sea in another twenty years, with any luck the rude gawpers and nasty drivers would get washed out to sea as well.

Thelonious eventually found himself at the top of the village high street. By now his stomach was rumbling something awful, but he felt certain there was a pint with his name on it, not to mention a big slice of Shepherd's Pie and chips waiting for him in one of the local pubs. He couldn't wait to take a load off—his camera bag had begun to feel like he had an anchor hanging from his shoulder.

Wickham Marsh boasted a tourist office, a women's clothing shop, a greengrocer, a butcher, a baker, a souvenir shop selling T-shirts and the usual tat, an ice cream parlour, a café, a newsagent's/post office, and an arts and crafts gallery featuring the work of local artisans. The village also boasted two pubs, one of which was located in a white-washed hotel at the bottom of the road overlooking the fen. The other, which Thelonious resolutely made his way toward, was halfway down the hill. A sign hanging above the door read The Fat Badger, its comically obese mascot grinning like a loon from the painted board. With a name like that, the place was guaranteed to be overflowing with character, not to mention some good Norfolk ale!

A number of people were milling about outside the pub. Thelonious reckoned it was the smokers or else an overflow from the lunch crowd. He hoped for the former, since he didn't want to be stuck waiting around for a table. As he got nearer, he saw that the majority of those gathered in front of The Fat Badger were police constables. The sight of their uniforms set off a churning in his gut—a churning which became worse when an all-too-familiar voice carried over to him above the low rumble of conversation. "Well, look who we have here!"

Thelonious wanted to run back up the hill, but he knew he'd never be able to outrun DCI Sidebottom, whose legs were longer than his, as was the reach of his determination to make his life a misery. "If yew fancy a pint, I suggest yew head to the hotel," the inspector quipped with his usual misplaced jocularity, closing the gap between them and eliminating any chance of a pretence at short-sightedness on Thelonious's part.

Sidebottom ran his palm over his balding pate, as if checking for new growth, his broad features registering disappointment. He seemed torn between Thelonious and whatever it was taking place behind him. Several of the police constables broke away from the others gathered on the pavement and went inside the pub, inadvertently providing an answer for Thelonious's unvoiced question as to why he couldn't buy his pint from The Fat Badger.

Either yellow police tape had suddenly become *de rigueur* in Norfolk villages or…

"'Fraid ol' Ollie Wickett bit the dust," said Sidebottom cheerfully, as if reporting that he'd just won the EuroMillions jackpot. "Owned The Fat Badger for as long as anyone can remember, even from before I was born."

"Ollie Wickett?" echoed Thelonious, his tongue thick in his mouth. The churning in his gut grew worse.

The inspector jabbed a thumb behind him, indicating the cordoned-off pub. "Publican," he explained, his tone suggesting that Thelonious should have already known that. "Owned The Fat Badger for donkey's years."

"And he's dead?"

"Sure as I'm stood here." The DCI paused as if to reflect

on the matter, his farmer's face crumpling with what appeared to be the onset of tears. Regaining his composure, he narrowed his eyes, glaring at Thelonious with suspicion. "Why? Did yew know him?"

"No, I didn't know him. How could I know him? I've never even been here before!" Thelonious was feeling boxed in and panicky and must've looked it too, because a couple of the police constables had suddenly taken to watching him with keen interest. Great. This was just what he needed. It was a good thing he didn't have a garden, because the way things were going, they'd be digging it up looking for bodies.

"Keep your hat on, *Ted*. Yew don't want your blood pressure to go playing up."

Thelonious reached up to check that his beloved deerstalker was still in place, relieved when his paws connected with fabric instead of fur. He immediately felt foolish.

"High blood pressure can lead to a heart attack," the inspector added helpfully.

Blood pressure? Heart attack? Did Sidebottom moonlight as a cardiology consultant for the National Health Service when he wasn't out harassing innocent citizens? Why did the mere presence of the man make Thelonious feel guilty? He'd never done anything criminal in his life—or at least not since stealing a jar of honey when he was a cub (and his mother had made him return it to the Indian shopkeeper immediately afterward!). He was a clean-living bear. He just wanted a quiet life. But the DCI was like a hungry dog with a big juicy bone in his teeth—and Thelonious had become that bone.

One of the PCs who'd been eyeing him came over. "Everything all right, guv?" he asked the inspector, staring down at Thelonious with an expression wavering between amusement and disbelief. Without waiting for a reply, he whispered something into Sidebottom's ear. The DCI nodded, at which point the constable re-joined the others. A moment later laughter rang out and they turned to look at Thelonious, nudging each other playfully with their elbows.

Thelonious felt like running over and kicking them in their kneecaps. Where did they hire these people from—the local primary school? He expected better, especially from those who'd been placed in a position that required them to respectfully serve and protect the public. Though if DCI Sidebottom was a shining example of—.

"How long yew been in Wickham Marsh for?" The inspector's eyes once again bored into Thelonious, a hawk sighting its prey. "Thought yew were stopping at Little Acre?"

Thelonious's jaw moved up and down as if some madman controlled it with strings, eventually regaining enough control of it to croak: "I came for the day."

"How's that?"

"I came for the day!" he repeated more sharply than he'd intended.

Sidebottom's back went rigid as a board, his features hardening along with it. "Still at Mrs. Baxter's then?"

Thelonious nodded. All he wanted was to be back behind the steering wheel of his Mini Cooper, with Wickham Marsh a distant spec on the horizon and DCI Horatio Sidebottom of the Norfolk Constabulary Criminal Investigations Department an even more distant spec on his memory. So much for his grand day out in the Fens and all his excitement about starting a new life here. At this rate he wouldn't need to bother about renting a cottage—he'd be able to get free accommodation in Norfolk at Her Majesty's Pleasure. Hopefully the prison cells came with a view.

Sidebottom glanced over his shoulder at The Fat Badger, then returned his attention to Thelonious. "We don't get murders round these parts."

Thelonious wondered how many more corpses needed to turn up before Lieutenant Columbo here came to the realisation that they *did* get murders round these parts. Not that he was any expert on criminal investigations, but it was beginning to sound like Norfolk had a serial killer in its midst—a serial killer with a serious aversion to village publicans. Maybe the DCI should let Lord Nelson take over the case, since the man didn't seem competent enough to solve a child's crossword. Why, even Thelonious could probably do a better job of it. Perhaps if the photojournalism work dried up, he'd do a bit of moonlighting as a sleuth. He nearly chuffed with laughter at the idea until the inspector's next words cut it off before it could begin.

"I expect yew to keep me informed when yew decide to move on." The DCI's once-jovial tone had turned coldly official.

Thelonious couldn't believe what he was hearing. "Are you saying I'm not allowed to leave the county?" The moment the words were out of his mouth he regretted them. Now for sure he'd cast himself in the role of "a person of interest." Yet what other reason could Sidebottom have for telling him that he wanted to be kept informed should he wish to leave?

The DCI's response confirmed his fears. "I'd prefer it if yew remained in the area."

Thelonious told himself to remain calm. He'd done nothing wrong; therefore he had nothing to worry about.

At least he hoped he didn't.

Chapter Nine

Vinnie was well chuffed about the Fens job and felt like doing a bit of celebrating down the pub. Maybe after some pints he'd pull a couple of birds and have it off with them at the same time. He'd always wanted to do that and reckoned he could manage it fine without missing a beat. A few drinks and these birds were up for anything—and he had plenty of dosh in his pocket to pay for a few drinks and even some blow, should they fancy it. Seemed that Wickett geezer had taken in a nice bit of dosh the day the brothers had offed him. Vinnie saw it as a Christmas bonus, even though it was summer and even though he'd never had the sort of jobs that paid their workers such things as Christmas bonuses. Not that he'd ever been employed in *any* sort of job—at least not the ones that came with a wage packet the Inland Revenue and national insurance got their stinking hands on.

With this windfall in addition to the fee paid to them, Vinnie had to wonder why his brother had been going about with a face like a slapped arse. Finally he couldn't stand it anymore. "Oi! What's eatin' ya, bruv?" he said to Desmond as they were watching a reality series on the telly. Vinnie liked the programme, especially that blonde Essex bird with the big tits. Yeah, he knew they were all pumped up with jelly, but who gave a toss when you got results like that? The fact that she was always wearing those thong bikini bottoms and a top no bigger than a couple of Elastoplasts...well, things couldn't get any sweeter!

Desmond looked like a kid who'd just taken a dump in his pants and been caught out by his schoolmates. "Err...nothin', Vinnie," he stammered, refusing to move his eyes off the telly.

"*Nothin'*? Don't look like nothin' from where I'm sat." Vinnie thought his brother seemed awfully interested in watching that TV programme all of a sudden, especially since he was always banging on about how these reality shows were turning the minds of the British public into mush. Where he got off being so high and mighty and sounding like that Stephen Fry twat he'd no idea. Must've been all those poncey ready-meals they'd been eating. They gave Vinnie a right case of the shits. So they got them for free, big deal. The money they saved on food they were now spending on bog roll. It was a wonder he had any skin left in the crack of his arse.

"Oi! I'm talkin' to ya!" Vinnie shouted above the squeals coming from the blonde as some bloke tried to get her to eat a giant barbecued lizard. She was jumping up and down like she had a hive of red ants up her arse, her tits jouncing and wobbling so much Vinnie nearly shot his load from watching them...until he remembered his knob-head brother. "So why ya got the 'ump?"

"I ain't got the 'ump!" cried Desmond, bolting up from the sofa like a jack-in-the-box. He disappeared into the kitchen, where he began to rattle around as if he had some big clean-up to do from their evening meal, though it was only a couple of plastic cartons from the microwave that needed chucking in the bin, along with some tins of lager.

Nevertheless, he filled the plastic washing-up bowl with Fairy liquid and hot water, taking his time washing the two forks and two knives that *wouldn't* be going into the bin. While he was at it, he decided to give the kettle a good scrub as well. It had so much lime scale caked up inside of it that he feared for the state of his innards. Not that this was his only fear.

Truth be told, Desmond was worried. He needed his share of the money in hand, *not* under Vinnie's thumb. All this being partners and all—it was getting so they were married from the way Vinnie carried on. Did his brother think they could go on like this forever, living in each other's pockets? Desmond wanted his own life already. He wanted out of the business, *and* out of London. For one thing, he wasn't getting any younger. There'd come a day when the stress of the job would get to be too much for him. That's what had happened with their old man—heart gave out on him right in the middle of a job. Geezer whose electronics shop he'd been robbing found him the next morning on opening up. He also found his van parked in the alley out back, its rear doors still open, the interior filled with stereos and TVs from his shop.

Reggie Clark had died before his time, leaving his two young sons to fend for themselves. Sure, they'd done all right, but by then they'd already left school and were doing their own jobs. Though maybe if their old man had still been around, they'd never have ended up in the nick. For that Desmond blamed Vinnie. And he knew Vinnie blamed *him*. It was a blame game neither of them won.

He had to get his hands on that dosh. But how to do it without making his brother suspicious as to why he suddenly needed it? Up till now they'd been putting everything into the kitty, taking out a bit for this and that, never anything major. For Desmond to follow through on his master plan he needed a big fat wad of cash deposited into an offshore account in his name, which he could then use to draw on as needed once he was in the Costa Brava. How was he expected to live if he didn't have any money to live *on*?

Vinnie came swaggering into the kitchen and stood in the doorway. "Don't know what's up with ya lately, bruv, but I don't like it."

Desmond could feel his brother's rat's eyes boring a hole into his back and his hands froze in the tepid dishwater. He didn't want to turn around, because if he did, Vinnie would know everything just from seeing his face. Hell, he probably already knew everything, though how that could be possible Desmond had no idea. He hadn't told anyone about his plans. The only thing he'd done was use the internet at the public library to search for properties to rent—and he doubted Vinnie had ever been anywhere near a public library, let alone a computer. His brother might've been good with his hands, but upstairs he was thick as an effing plank.

"So ya gonna tell me what's eatin' ya or what?"

Setting the sponge he'd been using to clean the kettle with onto the draining board, Desmond turned around. Rather than meeting Vinnie's washed-out blue eyes full on, he made a big show of tidying the small Formica-topped table they rarely used for meals, diligently sweeping non-existent crumbs into his hand. "Ain't nothin' eatin' me, Vin."

"Ya sure about that?"

"I'm just tired is all. We been goin' at it like gangbusters the last few weeks. Guess I ain't as young as I used to be." Desmond attempted a laugh, but it came out a strangled cry.

Vinnie squinted uncertainly at his brother, then seemed to lighten up. "Yeah, ya got that right. Me back's been playin' up something awful since that Pickles geezer. Been wonderin' if maybe I should get a massage with one of them Oriental birds. And while she's at it she can give the ol' todger a massage, too!"

"Yeah, that's the ticket," Desmond agreed, wishing his brother would start getting it regular so he could have more time on his own to plan his escape. It was like they were a pair of Siamese twins. He couldn't even take a piss without Vinnie lurking nearby.

"Maybe we need to have ourselves a little holiday," said

Vinnie. "I hear the Costa Brava's real nice this time a year."

Desmond felt the shit freeze in his bowels. He allowed himself to look his brother full in the eye. But there was nothing there to see—nothing to indicate he was on to him. Vinnie looked like the same old tosser of a Vinnie. "Yeah," he mumbled, not knowing what else to say that wouldn't land him in it. The thought of taking a holiday with Vinnie—especially to the Costa Brava—was enough to put him in the grave with their old man.

"Soon's we get this last job out of the way we can grab us some chill time." Vinnie stuck his head inside the fridge to get a tin of lager. Popping it open, he emptied half of it down his throat, belching with satisfaction. "Wouldn't mind goin' to that island where that blonde bird off the telly is. Bet she'll be bendin' over and touchin' her toes real quick when she gets a load of this!" He grabbed his crotch. "Prime British beef, ay? Ain't nothin' better!" Finishing off the rest of his lager, Vinnie grabbed a replacement and left the kitchen. A moment later Desmond heard the pop of the tin being opened, followed by a "*Phwoar!* Look at them tits!".

Seemed he'd got a reprieve. But for how long?

Chapter Ten

THELONIOUS DECIDED TO LIE LOW and avoid The Drowned Duck for a while. His latest run-in with his favourite gumshoe had put him right off the idea of going. He'd either find somewhere else to have his pint and evening meal or stay locked inside his room like a prisoner until daybreak. Since he was already being treated like a criminal by Norfolk Constabulary CID, it wouldn't be much of a stretch to live like one. Thelonious didn't want to place himself further in the line of fire on what had now become his home turf (at least temporarily)—not when DCI Sidebottom probably lived right around the corner. It seemed unlikely the inspector would choose to drink in the village unless he actually lived here. Little Acre wasn't exactly a major draw for non-locals—and judging by the emptiness of Baxter House's car park, it wasn't a major draw for tourists either. Unless tourists were interested in rubbing elbows with the high society from the village's only public house, there wasn't a whole lot to attract them to Little Acre.

Which was what made the pub so appealing. It existed within its own quirky little bubble uninfluenced by tourism or spoiled Londoners looking to create another version of what they already had. Thelonious liked The Drowned Duck with its reasonably priced food and oddball characters and bad music. He was even developing a fondness for Lord Nelson. Having to avoid the place because of some pesky policeman didn't seem at all fair.

Therefore when he learned from Mrs. Baxter that the inspector did *not*, in fact, reside in Little Acre but several villages away in Abbey Knoll—"out Norwich way," she'd said—Thelonious felt as if someone had given him a *Get Out of Jail Free* card. When the landlady added that the DCI lived in a "darling little cottage with his wife and their cats" (her nose wrinkling with distaste on the "wife" part), he had to wonder how she knew so much about the man's personal business. Thelonious couldn't imagine the landlady of a village bed and breakfast having much in common with a detective chief inspector—not unless they compared notes on which brand of tinned beans was the cheapest and most indigestible rubbish to serve at breakfast. Not that DCI Sidebottom looked the sort to open a tin of *anything*, let alone bother with such mundane tasks as preparing meals when he had a wife at home to do it for him.

As for the ever-informative Mrs. Baxter, Thelonious had yet to catch a glimpse of her elusive and oft-spoken about husband. When he recalled Sidebottom's earlier ale-induced praise of the landlady's apparent charms, Mr. Baxter's absence took on even greater significance. In fact, it conjured up all sorts of scenarios in Thelonious's mind, none of which he wished to dwell on.

With DCI Sidebottom no longer a significant local threat, Thelonious considered it safe to resume his nightly visits to The Drowned Duck, where he partook of his heart's content of buttered samphire and Norfolk ale. Despite the time that had gone by since his last visit, everything was the same—from the bar-side bonhomie of Fag-stain Man and his sticky companion the beekeeper to old windypops himself Lord Nelson, who'd now taken up singing (which helped drown out Barry Manilow), the talent becoming particularly evident when combined with the seduction of a patron's leg. The dog didn't discriminate—Thelonious had to give him that. Whether the leg was attached to a man or woman, the mangy cur put forth the same amount of effort in the romance department, though he never got any satisfaction. It reminded Thelonious of the classic rock song from the Sixties, which, in turn, reminded him of where he knew Fag-stain Man from.

The Belgians and their belching Russian companion were seated in a huddle at their usual table, and the vicar and his wife at theirs, neither displaying an inclination to engage with each other save for the occasional glare. The publican held court behind the bar, waving about his latest bit of road-kill, which Thelonious concluded would end up on the next day's menu. Even the grand entrance of Zimmer-frame Granny with its accompanying crescendo of banging and crashing had become a nightly ritual, along with the whisky-drinking competition between her and Fag-stain Man. Thelonious was comforted by the fact that nothing at The Drowned Duck ever changed. And now he too, had become part of the scenery.

The following Sunday Thelonious returned to Kelton Market, since he wanted to get some photos of market day. He'd decided to concentrate on general images to capture a sense of local colour rather than photographing the individual faces of customers and traders. It was easier not to bother with getting release forms signed. Thelonious had found that people weren't always that cooperative when it came to giving permission for their images to potentially be used in print. Indeed, they could be downright belligerent, especially these testy market traders. You'd have thought he was trying to steal their souls from the way they carried on. He'd never forget that time in Portobello Market when some dreadlocked

Rastafarian selling what were probably counterfeit DVDs demanded to be paid fifty pounds just for having his hand appear in a shot. Thelonious had refused, and quite rightly so!

Kelton Market was bustling and it took an eternity for him to find parking, but Thelonious was determined to get this done once and for all. The market had been set up in the centre of the village, with most of the high street blocked off to allow traders to ply their wares and customers to mill about without fear of motorists mowing them down, so he had to walk some distance before he found himself in the midst of the action. Despite the village's snobby veneer, there was a sense of fun in the air that hadn't been there on his previous visit, making him glad he'd decided to return. Kelton Market gave no indication that it had recently been the scene of a murder. Even the yellow police tape cordoning off the entrance to The Black Stag had been removed. Everything looked normal, except for the fact that the pub wasn't open for business on what should have been a busy lunchtime when people would want their Sunday roasts. The thought of a nice joint of beef with all the trimmings made Thelonious' stomach rumble with hunger…

…Until he noticed the large banner draped across the pub's façade.

> THE LADY ROSE
> A PAOLO LOUIS BLACK PUB
> GRAND OPENING IN SEPTEMBER!

Thelonious could not believe his eyes. Derrick Pickles's corpse hadn't even been given time to cool off and already his pub had been sold! It appeared that the wheels of commerce turned very quickly in these parts. Suddenly he recalled reading in the local newspaper about the publican being survived by a son; he'd probably decided to offload the place rather than take it over. Having had first-hand experience with The Pheasant Inn in Hunters Cove, Thelonious didn't plan to celebrate the grand opening of the celebrity chef's newest gastro-venture. The random eccentricities of The Drowned Duck were good enough for him and his wallet, thank you very much.

To his surprise, Thelonious found himself enjoying the atmosphere of the market, though he didn't enjoy the attention he attracted—especially since he was trying to work. One little boy kept breaking away from his mother to run up and pull at his fur, asking Thelonious if he was stuffed with sawdust. The fact that the halfwit who'd given birth to the creature hadn't seen fit to discipline him made Thelonious want to do the task himself, though he knew the minute he'd lay a paw on the brat the mother would be shrieking bloody murder. It amazed him that prospective parents weren't required to pass an aptitude test to prove they were fit to be parents. You didn't see this sort of thing in the ursine community. A cub would *never* have been allowed to get away with such bad behaviour.

Thelonious relocated himself to safety and away from the boy's line of sight, inadvertently placing himself *within* the line of sight of the bespoke clothiers' window. The shop was open for business and actually had a customer. He watched as the young man who apparently had money to burn stretched out his arms while another man flew about with a tape measure, ducking out of view, reappearing, then dropping out of view again, his head bobbing up and down in front of the customer. Had Thelonious not seen the tape measure, he might've concluded that something very rude was taking place, considering the proximity of the salesman's head to the customer's nether regions. Suddenly the salesman came back into view again and turned to face the window, looking directly at Thelonious.

Although he was standing some distance away, Thelonious couldn't fail to recognise that pencil nose. Unable to resist the opportunity, he stuck his paw up in the air and executed a two-clawed salute, baring his teeth. When he was assured by the outrage on the salesman's face that he'd taken note of the salutation, Thelonious turned to make his getaway, only to run head on into the bane of his existence.

"Ted!" greeted DCI Sidebottom, sounding as if he'd encountered a long-lost friend. Seeing Thelonious's camera, he added: "I see you're out enjoying the sights."

Thelonious shifted his heavy camera bag farther back on his shoulder so that it would be less obvious. Better to maintain the guise of a tourist rather than answer more impertinent questions. Not that anything would stop the inspector from his never-ending quest to probe into Thelonious's private business.

"The wife's always on at me to bring her down the market." The DCI gestured with a jerk of his balding head toward a gaggle of women at a stall picking over some pottery. Thelonious gathered that one of them must be Mrs. Sidebottom—probably the dowdy one with the wide hips. "Just seemed easier to load her into the car than argue."

For a moment Thelonious wasn't sure whether the inspector was referring to his wife or a box of household rubbish that needed to be taken to the tip. When the dowdy female shopper at the pottery stall turned toward them and waved in the air what had to be the ugliest flower pot on the planet, he had his answer: they were one and the same. Sidebottom gave her a dismissive wave and returned his attention to Thelonious. "Guess I'll be needing to get out my cash card," he added with a good-natured chuckle.

The inspector seemed to be in fine spirits and Thelonious wondered when the proverbial would be hitting the fan, since no encounter with DCI Sidebottom had been absent of at least one mention of murder and mayhem. Not wanting to break the happy spell that had been placed on the inspector, he kept silent, hoping that Mrs. Sidebottom would come drag her hapless spouse off to look at lace doilies. Judging by the pottery she preferred, the doily hawker should have something equally unsightly upon which to place it.

"Expect yew noticed The Black Stag is under new ownership."

Here it comes, thought Thelonious, steeling himself. His

camera bag was beginning to feel like a barbell on his shoulder, but he didn't want to set it down, nor did he want to alert Sidebottom of its presence by shifting it to the other shoulder. The man would probably want to search it for weapons. Or drugs. So he suffered in silence, knowing there'd be hell to pay later with his back.

"I'm not one for these fancy new pubs," continued the inspector, his farmer's face scowling in disapproval. "A pub should be a pub. The sun might've set on the great British Empire, but pubs? Now *that* we do better than anyone else!"

Thelonious let down his guard ever so slightly. Maybe Sidebottom wasn't out to get him today. Maybe he'd finally realised just how ridiculous it was to keep hounding him for something he couldn't possibly have had any part in.

"It's not right that some outsider should come waltzing in here and take over like that. Not right at all."

On that point Thelonious was in total agreement. He'd been seeing the gastropub craze taking over London and steadily eroding the essence of what a pub was meant to be. Apparently he and his flat-footed nemesis both recognised the dangers of this recent phenomenon, particularly when it came to these rural villages. He'd have thought the local councils would have been more concerned about preserving the character and integrity of their parishes rather than allowing them to be turned into miniature versions of London. But then, it was all about money. It always was.

Just as Thelonious was getting ready to put in his tuppence worth on the subject, the inspector stared pointedly at him and said: "Derrick Pickles was a good man."

Thelonious's gut went into a clench-lock. He already knew what was coming next.

"We don't get murders round these parts."

Chapter Eleven

"One more job, bruv, and that's it."

Desmond was unconvinced. With Vinnie Clark it was never "one more" of anything, not when there was money involved. "Just don't feel right about it, Vin."

Vinnie sneered. "*Don't feel right about it?*" he mimicked in a high girly voice. "Why ya makin' such a fuss all of a sudden? Ya goin' soft on me or what?"

"I ain't goin' soft!"

"Then where's your bottle? It's so easy it's like nickin' sweets off a babe."

The Clark brothers occupied their usual places on the sofa in front of the wide-screen TV, where a football match was in progress. Desmond hated it when his brother was like this. Vinnie had been in a right strop to begin with. He got that way every time he saw Carlos Tévez play, never having forgiven him for leaving West Ham United. "Fuckin' pikey traitor!" he'd shout whenever Tévez came on the telly or was mentioned in passing. It had got him into some close scrapes down the local, since not everyone shared his opinion.

Desmond picked at a hangnail, unwilling to look at his brother since he knew Vinnie would see the truth in his eyes. "Yeah. Maybe it's *too* easy," he replied, hoping to divert attention from the *real* reason behind his reluctance—he just wanted out. No more Vinnie, no more killing, no more nothing. He wanted the Costa Brava—and he wanted it *now*.

"Don't know what's gettin' into ya lately. Ya just ain't the same Des no more." Vinnie shook his shaved head in disgust at both his brother and Tévez, neither of whom were in his good books at the moment. "Ya turnin' into some nancy, what with them posh toff ready-meals. I know we get that dog puke for free. Don't mean we gotta eat it though."

"I ain't turnin' into no nancy!" cried Desmond, only to back down when he saw a flash of menace on Vinnie's face. "But a bloke's gotta change sometime, Vin. Can't expect to stay the same forever. Maybe it ain't so smart for us to be takin' risks like this no more. We don't got years ahead of us to waste in the nick if we get banged up again."

"We ain't gonna get banged up, ya tit! Besides, I already gave the geezer my word we'd do it—and the word of a Clark is gold. I ain't goin' back on it now. I got a reputation to maintain."

Desmond clutched at mental straws, trying to find a way out of the situation. "So how about usin' one of the lads instead, like Tommy Newton?"

Vinnie snorted. "*That* tosser? Ya daft or what? I ain't usin' no Tommy Newton."

"Then how about that Den Watson?" Desmond knew he was pushing his luck, but he was bricking it at the thought of doing another job with his brother. Though Vinnie was right about it being dead easy, that didn't do much to reassure him. Maybe he was getting paranoid in his old age. Or maybe it was like his brother said and he *was* losing his bottle.

"Like I said, bruv, we can take some time off after this next one, yeah? We got plenty to splash about on booze and birds—I reckon we deserve a bit of fun after workin' so hard," said Vinnie, his tone suddenly placating. "I already got in our intelligence from them geezers up in Norfolk and we're set to roll."

Intelligence? Had the Clark brothers joined MI5? Either Vinnie had been watching too many of them James Bond films or else he was losing it, full stop. "Ya sure this is gonna be the last one?" asked Desmond, knowing when to admit defeat. His hangnail had begun to bleed and his stuck the tip of his finger into his mouth, the metallic taste of blood bringing back the memory of the smashed-in skull of the bloke they'd offed in the Fens.

"That's what I said, innit. We signed on for three jobs. One, two…and what comes after two?"

"Three."

"Right. Three."

"And you're sure them geezers in Norfolk are spot on?"

"They been spot on the last two times. What makes ya think they ain't gonna be spot on this time?"

"Guess I just like to see who I'm workin' with is all."

"I ain't too crazy about dealing with no foreign geezers neither. If I had my way, I'd stay well clear of 'em, 'specially them pikey Russians. But it weren't my decision to make, was it?"

Desmond nodded. "S'pose you're right, Vinnie."

"'Course I'm right, ya daft twat! Now put the kettle on, will ya? I'm gaggin' for a cuppa."

Desmond had allowed himself to be led by his brother *again*. He might as well put a ring in his nose. Well, this was going to be the last time. Soon as it was over and done with, he would be claiming his share of the dosh and heading for the Costa Brava. And if Vinnie didn't like it….

Without another word, Desmond headed into the kitchen to sort their cups of tea. Flipping up the kettle's plastic lid, he frowned at the chunks of lime scale that had collected on the metal heating element at the bottom. He'd just given the effing thing a good scrub a few days ago. He shook his head in disgust, filling the kettle with water from the tap. He couldn't be bothered anymore. Besides, he'd be out of here soon enough.

"Now where'd I put that fuckin' thing?" grumbled Vinnie, startling his brother when he suddenly appeared behind him in the kitchen. Desmond hated it when Vinnie snuck up on him like that, like he was hoping to catch him doing something he shouldn't be doing. Vinnie pulled open the pantry door and began to root around, making plenty of noise as he shifted some cases of lager out of the way, eventually coming out with a sparkling new tyre iron that had been bought for what Desmond mentally referred to as *Job Number 3*. "Got ya, cheeky little bugger!" shouted Vinnie, his voice filled with affection. Had Desmond not seen what his brother held in his hand and known what it was intended for, he might've thought Vinnie had been searching for the family cat. If they had a cat, that is. Better they shouldn't have pets in the house—not with Vinnie's short fuse.

Vinnie held up the tyre iron for his brother's inspection. "What a thing of beauty, eh?" he said, grinning in a way that creeped Desmond out.

Desmond occupied himself with the business of spooning sugar into their mugs of tea, followed by milk. He passed a mug to Vinnie while gulping down the hot liquid from his own, his blood feeling like ice water. The sooner he got away from his psycho brother, the better. He just hoped he could hold it together till then.

Chapter Twelve

THE SOON-TO-BE OPENED PUB IN Kelton Market along with its celebrity TV chef owner Paulo Louis Black had become the featured topic of conversation at The Drowned Duck. Everyone seemed to hold the opinion that The Lady Rose was a slap in the face to long-time residents of the area, to say nothing of being a slap in the face to the late Derrick Pickles's memory. Although nearly no one in Little Acre actually went to the neighbouring village, they had plenty to say about what went on there.

By now Thelonious had begun to feel like a regular part of the scene and had even taken to hanging around by the bar, where he chimed in with his own thoughts on the subject, which happened to be in agreement with those already in existence. This ingratiated him no end with Fagstain Man, who clapped him on the shoulder and made sure the pints kept coming, all references to shandy apparently forgotten. Even the vicar and his wife showed a few signs of life, though not with each other. Instead they discussed this latest turn of events with the publican, who'd taken to joining them at their table with his latest road-kill, which he set onto a spare chair. The thing looked so forlorn sitting there that Thelonious felt like ordering it a pint. The regular presence of pheasant on the menu was undoubtedly a boon for the pub's profit margins and he wondered if it was owing to sheer bad luck on the part of the pheasant population or something more sinister, such as deliberate vehicular manslaughter with The Drowned Duck's publican behind the wheel.

The only patrons that didn't display any interest in joining the discussion were the three Belgians and their Russian cohort, all of whom preferred to remain in a huddle at their table, speaking their usual jumble of French and Russian. Well, them and Lord Nelson, who clearly had better things to occupy his time, such as trying to seduce Thelonious's leg until the filthy cur's owner finally scooped him up and took him into the back, where the creature spent the remainder of the evening howling out back-up vocals to "Copacabana" and various other Barry Manilow hits. Thelonious found it actually improved the music—and since no one had seen fit to shush the dog, it appeared everyone in the pub concurred.

"Just who does this Paulo Louis Whatsit think he is?" cried Zimmer-frame Granny, her wizened old face turning a shade of red that might have had more to do with the glasses of whisky she'd been tossing back than her anger over the situation. "He's no Jamie Oliver!" She slammed the rubber-tipped feet of the metal frame down onto the floor in emphasis, oblivious to any toes that were in the vicinity. "He's nothing but an ageing playboy! Besides that, he's ginger!" She screwed up her features in disgust.

"And he's not even from Norfolk!" added the beekeeper, both sounding and looking on the verge of tears. He swiped at his eyes with the sleeve of his white beekeeper suit, prompting a comforting pat on the back from Fag-stain Man, who signalled the Goth barmaid for the young man's pint to be replenished.

"This would never have happened if Pickles' spoiled city boy of a son had done right by his father and claimed what was lawfully his, not gone running off like a thief with the money!" continued the old woman. "These young people—" she shook her small grey head in dismay, "—they got no sense of values or tradition. Why, in my day—"

"What I don't get is how fast it all happened," interrupted Fag-stain Man, chewing on a nicotine-flavoured fingernail. "Pickles is barely cold and already his pub's been sold off."

"Oh, that's because his son was the legal owner," explained the old granny. "Few years back he convinced his father to sign it over to him to avoid inheritance taxes. Pretty sharp, if you ask me." Her rheumy eyes took on an unwholesome gleam. "And pretty convenient, considering…"

When Thelonious remarked that perhaps those who stood to profit the most from the publican's death should be looked at more closely as potentially having a hand in it, all eyes turned to him. Everyone began to nod and he could see their minds working to determine who the most viable murder suspect was. Too bad DCI Sidebottom wasn't here, mused Thelonious, especially since the man didn't seem to be very skilled when it came to crime solving. If Thelonious had been in charge of the investigation, he would've begun by having a criminal profile compiled in the event a serial killer was on the loose, what with the recent murder of the publican in Wickham Marsh. He'd also be questioning those individuals who had the most to gain from the deaths. Though maybe he was selling the inspector short and these things were already being done. In which case, that should put paid to any further harassment of him from that quarter.

Another glass of whisky materialised on the bar courtesy of Fag-stain Man. He passed it to the old woman, who snatched it from him with a palsied hand, downing it in one go. She smacked her withered lips together with relish, returning the empty glass to the bar. By Thelonious's count, it had to have been her fourth and he wondered how she could still manage to remain vertical. He would've been flat on his back after only the one. "It's a damned shame," she resumed, eliciting much nodding of heads from the beekeeper and her generous benefactor of spirits, who knocked back the contents of his own glass as if the whisky were no stronger than the local elderflower cordial.

Having gone in the back to check on the still-vocalising Lord Nelson, the publican returned to reclaim the dead pheasant from the vicar's table, whereupon he headed over to the bar to join the conversation, the bird swinging from his hand nearly whacking Thelonious on the head as it went past. Fortunately his quick reflexes allowed him to grab his deerstalker in time before it was knocked to the floor. "I expect old Pickles is turning in his grave as we speak," said the publican, his expression suitably grim. "If you ask me, that whole village has gone to rack and ruin what with all them Londoners taking over. And now we got Paulo Louis Black opening another of his fancy gastro-whatchamacallits on our doorstep? It's a damned disgrace, that's what it is!"

"He's no Jamie Oliver!" repeated Zimmer-frame Granny, her words becoming progressively slurred. "That Jamie is a good lad. He wouldn't be putting up prices like some rich Arab oil sheikh!"

Thelonious wanted to know how the old woman could possibly be privy to what Jamie Oliver would or would not do, to say nothing of being privy to the activities of rich Arab oil sheikhs when it was unlikely she'd been outside the confines of Little Acre in the last quarter of a century, except maybe in an ambulance.

"But Jamie Oliver isn't from Norfolk!" interjected the beekeeper, becoming upset all over again, his red-rimmed eyes shining with a fresh supply of tears.

"Paulo Louis Black..." said the old granny with a shrivelled sneer. "So who's he when he's at home? And he's ginger, too!"

At some point during the conversation the three Belgians and the Russian had gone very quiet at their table and appeared to be listening intently to what was being discussed, though they made no effort to participate. On the contrary, their chairs scraped back as they rose to leave, skulking out the door as if they didn't want to attract attention. What with their behaviour and body language, they looked as if they were trying to sneak out without having paid their bar tab.

After last orders, which included a round for the house courtesy of Fag-stain Man, Thelonious was feeling no pain as he toddled back to the B&B, only to have his happy mood disintegrate on discovering that the wrought-iron garden chair was missing from its usual place by the front door. He couldn't imagine Mrs. Baxter having any legitimate reason to move it (or the invisible Mr. Baxter). So far the landlady had been quite good about accommodating his special needs, and since there didn't seem to be any other guests in residence that just left the possibility of theft. Not that anyone would find value in a rusty old iron chair with the paint peeling off (other than Mrs. Baxter). Nevertheless, it wasn't there. And if it wasn't there, that meant Thelonious couldn't reach high enough to unlock and open the door.

If a crime had been committed, perhaps he should summon DCI Sidebottom. Indeed, the image of the inspector racing over to Baxter House with police sirens blaring and several police constables in tow sent Thelonious into a fit of drunken chortles and he nearly lost his footing on the gravel as he backed up a few steps into the car park to see if any lights were on in the upstairs corner of the house where he'd determined Mrs. Baxter's bedroom to be located.

The window was dark; the landlady was likely tucked up in bed fast asleep wearing some awful flower-printed nightie. After all the ale Thelonious had been drinking at The Drowned Duck, he was in no fit state to deal with ladders, despite having one to hand in the boot of his Mini. Apparently he had no choice but to start banging on the door, since he also couldn't reach the bell. He just hoped the blasted woman would hear him. She looked like one of those people who slept like a bear in hibernation. As Thelonious envisioned her floral-printed bulk snoring peacefully in a cave decorated with Royal Family memorabilia, he was seized by yet another bout of drunken chortles. He'd really gone past his limit tonight with that Norfolk ale. He dreaded to think of the state of Zimmer-frame Granny, who was probably lying unconscious on the pavement outside The Drowned Duck, along with Fag-stain Man and the beekeeper.

Thelonious pressed his furry face to the glass panel alongside the door, hoping for a glimpse of life inside, but all he saw was the brightly patterned rug in the entry hall, along with the guestbook and a vase of plastic flowers on the sideboard. He supposed he should be grateful that Mrs. Baxter at least had left the light on. Some of these B&B owners shut off their interior lights after a certain hour, preferring that their guests break their necks as they tried to locate a wall switch rather than paying a few pennies more for the electric bill.

As he raised his paw in readiness to launch against the door, Thelonious heard the scrunching of tyres on the gravel behind him. He turned around, finding himself illuminated by the headlights of a Ford Fiesta as it slid between his Mini Cooper and the broken-down bicycle. All four doors flew open at once, followed by the appearance of four sets of denim-clad legs as the men they were attached to clambered out of the vehicle. They stretched their arms high above their heads as if they'd been inside the car for too long, punctuating the activity with a few groans, one of which turned into a belch that sounded very familiar.

Their shoes crunched noisily through the gravel of the car park as they made their way toward Thelonious. "*Bonjour*," mumbled the first of the party to reach the door. He removed a key from the pocket of his leather jacket and unlocked the door, holding it open so that Thelonious could go in first. The other three followed suit until all five of them were crowded into Baxter House's small entry hall. Thelonious could feel his jaw dropping open in shock. Had they been staying here all this time?

At that moment Mrs. Baxter materialised on the upstairs

landing in all her floral-printed finery. "Why, good evening, gentlemen!" she greeted, her broad face abloom with what Thelonious surmised was a surplus of female hormones likely caused by the absence of her husband—providing, of course, there actually *was* a husband. "Have you all met?" She made her way down the stairs with an attempt at queenly grace, thwarting any chance Thelonious had of making a quick escape up to his room—not unless he pushed her over the railing to move her out of the way.

"Mr. Bear, allow me to do the honours! Now let me make sure I have this right," she said, turning first to the man with the leather jacket. "François?" When he nodded, she continued to the next man. "Girard?" Another nod. "Jacques?" Yet another. "And last, but not least, Igor!" she finished with a flourish, opening her chubby arms outward like a stage performer about to take a bow. Igor acknowledged the landlady's talent for remembering names with one of his trademark belches, whereupon the quartet headed for the stairs, making it clear that their desire for social niceties had come to an end. Mrs. Baxter flattened herself as best she could against the railing, allowing the men to squeeze past.

As Thelonious attempted to follow suit, she blocked off his escape route. "I do hope you're enjoying your stay in Norfolk, Mr. Bear," she said. "You're always rushing off somewhere and we never have time for a proper natter!"

The idea of a proper natter with the landlady of Baxter House was not exactly high on Thelonious's list of priorities. However, it appeared to be high on Mrs. Baxter's. "Horatio speaks of you often," she continued, giving no indication as to who this Horatio person was or what he had to say or her feelings about whatever it was that he *had* said. "You've probably gathered by now that we're a close-knit little bunch in these parts!"

Baffled, Thelonious poked beneath his deerstalker hat to get at an itch as Mrs. Baxter prattled on. "You're probably wondering how Horatio and I know each other. Well…"

Horatio.

Suddenly everything became clear and Thelonious blamed his ale-addled brain for the slow uptake. The landlady meant Horatio—as in Detective Chief Inspector Horatio Sidebottom of the Norfolk Constabulary Criminal Investigations Department. The pieces were beginning to click into place, and he didn't much like the completed picture. All that good Norfolk ale he'd been enjoying all evening at The Drowned Duck courtesy of Fag-stain Man threatened to pay a return visit over Mrs. Baxter's floral-patterned bedroom slippers. Thelonious felt embarrassed and ashamed. The landlady probably thought she had Charles Manson sleeping under her roof, if DCI Sidebottom had anything to do with it.

"...So we go back years, as you can see."

Whatever their connection was, Thelonious had apparently just missed it—and he wasn't about to ask Mrs. Baxter to go back and explain it to him again. Nor would he ask what the inspector had been saying about him. Since the landlady hadn't grabbed up the nearest sharp object to defend herself with, he must be in the clear. Maybe this was finally the end of it and Sidebottom had found some other poor bastard to hound—or better yet, some *real* criminals to investigate.

Thelonious was dead on his feet and he yawned widely, knowing from experience that the sight of his choppers usually provided sufficient encouragement when he wanted to get rid of someone. "Oh!" cried Mrs. Baxter with a fair bit of alarm. "I see I'm keeping you from your bed." She began to back up on the stairs until she reached the landing, at which point she called down to him: "Have a good night's sleep, Mr. Bear. I'll see you in the morning at breakfast!" And with that, she vanished in a floral-printed haze.

Yawning yet again, Thelonious trudged wearily up to his room, puzzling over the fact that the four men from the pub were guests at Baxter House and had in all probability been staying at the B&B all along. He'd seen them—or at least he'd seen the three Belgians—the very first time he'd gone to The Drowned Duck, with the Russian turning up the following evening. He wondered what they were doing here, since they didn't look like typical tourists. Though, to be fair, neither did Thelonious, as DCI Sidebottom had so kindly reminded him. Maybe they were on one of those job-training courses—trainee sheep herders or beekeepers or something equally Norfolk-ish. That might explain why he'd never run into them at the B&B until tonight or seen their Ford Fiesta parked in the car park.

Still, he couldn't shake the feeling that something about the four was slightly off. Perhaps he should mention them to DCI Sidebottom the next time he saw him—not that the inspector was one for seeing the obvious. And it wasn't up to Thelonious to do the man's job for him.

Chapter Thirteen

VINNIE MANAGED TO KEEP TO THE posted speed limits, despite being all pumped up on adrenalin and wanting to floor it like a Formula One race car driver. He always did fancy himself a Tiff Needell sort of bloke and reckoned he'd be a real natural on the telly too. If things had been different and he hadn't come off a rough council estate and ended up in the nick, there was no telling where he'd be by now. The birds would've been coming out of the woodwork if he had the fame to go with the swagger! They all liked a bit of rough, especially them posh ones. Not that Vinnie Clark couldn't pull a posh bird if he had a mind to. He had plenty of rough to go around—and he didn't mind spreading the wealth either.

"Another job well done, ay, Des, me old son?" he chirped, feeling well chuffed with himself. The Clark brothers were in their white transit van, leaving the night-blackened Norfolk Broads behind them. "I feel higher'n a kite. Even got meself a stiffy, if ya can believe it!" he added with a laugh. "Think I'm gonna miss this place. Had some good times 'ere, we did."

Desmond shuddered. If bashing in some geezer's skull with a tyre iron till he snuffed it was "good times," then he was well out of it. "Sure, Vinnie, sure," he replied to fill up the space, knowing that silence would only irritate his brother and push him into another tirade about Desmond losing his bottle or being a nancy or whatever offence happened to be on the menu this week.

"Shame we don't got us some more jobs lined up, 'specially at this kinda dosh. We'd be able to retire anywhere we wanted after a few more."

"Yeah, but ya said this was the last one and—"

"Yeah, I know what I said—keep ya shirt on, bruv! I'm just thinkin' ahead is all. A bloke's gotta make plans for the future, yeah?"

Making plans for the future was what Desmond had been doing these last few months. *His* future, which didn't include Psycho Vinnie. "But I thought that posh toff just wanted us to do them three jobs? He didn't say nothin' about no others!" Desmond knew he was sounding like some panicky bint who'd been given the wrong colour nail varnish at the beauty salon and he tried to hold back his rising hysteria. If Vinnie thought they could off any more geezers in Norfolk and get away with it he was out of his effing gourd. No way could their luck continue. He was amazed it had even lasted *this* long.

"What we need are some more clients," said Vinnie, slapping the steering wheel as if he'd just solved the world debt crisis. "*Proper* clients who don't mind payin' for quality."

Desmond felt his bollocks shrivelling up as he sat in the passenger seat watching the night pass by outside the van's grimy windows. He didn't like where this conversation was headed. His brother was getting greedy; he should've known the temptation to pull in all this money would be too much for Vinnie to ignore. "So we got lucky with this posh geezer.

Don't mean it's gonna happen again," said Desmond, hoping to make him see sense.

Vinnie seemed not to hear him. "We're on our way up, bruv! Can't ya see it?"

"But Vinnie—"

"But nothin'. There ain't no stoppin' us now. The Clark brothers are gonna be fuckin' legends in this game! They'll be plasterin' our mugs on souvenir plates and hangin' 'em on the walls like we was the Queen!"

Desmond was more concerned about their mugs being plastered on *Crimewatch* from the telly. When Vinnie suddenly launched into an out-of-key chorus of "Don't Stop Me Now" by Queen, he wondered if his brother might be on something. Although he was always hyped up after a job, he was sounding like a right nutter. Desmond thought maybe he should have a nose around Vinnie's stuff when he was out of the house just to see if he found anything dodgy, like little packets of white powder or something. But then he figured, fuck it—he'd be out of here soon enough. If Vinnie wanted to go into self-demolition mode, let him. It wasn't Desmond's problem anymore. Or at least it wouldn't be his problem once he got his hands on his share of the money.

"Yeah, we're all done 'ere. But that ain't to say we won't be pullin' in more jobs like this. These just added to our portfolio, is all."

Portfolio? Where was Vinnie getting this shit from? It sounded like he wanted to sell shares on the stock market. Well, Desmond wasn't having it. He'd told himself this was the last time. He was washing his hands of any more killing. And he was washing his hands of Vinnie.

The Clarks' van pulled off the motorway just past Cambridge, barrelling toward the village of Grantchester. The brothers had mapped it all out ahead of time where they'd dump the tyre iron, not wanting to keep it with them any longer than they needed to. When they reached the Fen Causeway Bridge over the River Cam, Vinnie stopped the van in the middle and left the engine running. It was almost two in the morning. There was no sign of anyone about, no cars, nothing. Which was what they'd reckoned on.

Vinnie ordered Desmond out of the van. "Hurry up, ya twat!" he hissed as Desmond wrestled with the blanket-wrapped tyre iron stowed under the passenger seat. Finally he managed to wedge it loose. He took a quick look around, then tipped the blanket and its bloodied contents over the side of the bridge. Instead of the splash he'd been waiting for, he heard a dull *thunk*.

Desmond peered over the barrier to the water below. A punt that had broken loose from its moorings somewhere along the river had floated part of the way under the bridge. Even in the dark he was able to make out the lumpy shape of the blanket lying on the floor of the boat. Vinnie was going to kill him! But there was no way in hell he'd go wading into some mucky river to collect it. For one thing, he couldn't swim. For another…well, it just wasn't going to happen. It was too risky that someone would come along, especially local coppers who might wonder why a white transit van was parked on the bridge at two in the morning. Desmond wasn't about to go getting caught with a murder weapon in his hands while Vinnie legged it to safety. Brotherly love only went so far, especially where Vinnie Clark was concerned.

Suddenly he remembered Vinnie showing off the tyre iron in the kitchen a few days earlier—and he hadn't been wearing gloves when he'd handled it.

Desmond jumped back into the van as if someone had stuck a cattle prod up his jacksie, determined to keep schtum about what had happened. He was seriously bricking it. If anyone found that tyre iron, his brother's prints would be all over it, along with blood and bits of brain and skull belonging to the geezer in the Broads. But there was no point upsetting Vinnie, especially when there was nothing to be done for it. Maybe whoever found the thing would chuck it in the bin, not bothering to check what was wrapped inside, reckoning some homeless geezer had been using the blanket to sleep in. It did smell pretty rank. And it would smell a lot ranker once it started to cook in the morning sun, it being summer and all.

Once the brothers were safely back on the motorway headed for London, Vinnie didn't need to concentrate so much on the road. With one hand balanced on top of the steering wheel, he used the other to reach for the tin of Coke he'd helped himself to earlier at the pub. He'd also helped himself to some cases of lager, which were now stored in the back of the van along with several boxes containing packets of crisps, cheese and onion being his favourite. He liked a job that came with perks. "Find us some music, bruv," he said.

Grateful for the distraction, Desmond fiddled about with the radio tuner until he found a station he hoped wouldn't be playing all the usual top 40 and club mix rubbish. Since the adverts were still running, he couldn't tell what kind of music the station specialised in, though anything would be preferable to listening to more of Vinnie's big plans for their future together as the Murder, Incorporated of the East End. After an advert featuring some bloke with an Indian accent selling cheap car insurance, the music came on.

Vinnie exploded, spraying the windscreen with the Coke he hadn't yet swallowed. "What the fuck is that?" he shouted above a high-pitched female voice singing in Hindi.

"Sorry, Vinnie!" Desmond scrambled to reach the tuning button and, in his panic to avert another of his brother's outbursts, accidentally hit the volume control. The woman's voice keened at maximum strength in the van, rattling the speakers and windows and doors.

"For fuck's sake! Ya tryin' to blow out me earholes or what?" cried Vinnie.

Desmond moved to lower the volume, but the button refused to respond. He then tried to switch to another channel, which proved equally unsuccessful, as was shutting the thing off completely. The controls buttons were stuck fast in positions of permanently on, permanently loud, and permanently Bollywood.

The Clark brothers raced down the motorway toward home to the accompaniment of the latest Bollywood hits and a nonstop tirade of obscenities from the transit van's driver.

Chapter Fourteen

Local Publican Found Dead in Stanton Broad!
—Front page headline from the *BroadSheet*

THELONIOUS COULDN'T BELIEVE HOW quickly the time had passed since he'd arrived in Norfolk. He was already reaching the end of his assignment; he wasn't sure how much longer he could drag things out before he'd go over budget. His publisher hadn't exactly given him carte blanche to remain at a B&B indefinitely. He would need to sort out some proper accommodations soon or else he'd end up homeless. Perhaps it hadn't been such a brilliant idea to give up his London flat, but every time Thelonious was behind the wheel of his Mini zipping along a country lane with the wind in his fur and the wide-open Norfolk sky above, he knew he could never live in the capital again. With any luck, that charming peanut-brittle cottage in Wickham Marsh might still be available. If he rented it, at least then DCI Sidebottom couldn't accuse him of trying to leave town!

Although he'd amassed enough quality photos to fill *several* books, Thelonious still had one more place he wished to explore with his camera: the famous Norfolk Broads. Like an eagerly anticipated dessert, he'd been saving it for last. His plan was to hire one of those little motorised boats that putted along at a snail's pace. Not only would it be an enjoyable way to spend a few hours, it would provide him with a photographic perspective he couldn't achieve by any other means. He estimated a half day spent on the water should do it (weather permitting, of course), after which he'd check out the sights in the usual way, winding down the work day with a pint and meal in a local village pub. Hopefully he wouldn't stumble upon any more of Paulo Louis Black's gastro horrors. It seemed like the ginger-haired tycoon wanted to take over the entire county, if not the world!

Aside from the occasional rain shower, Thelonious had been pretty fortunate with the weather. Granted, Norfolk *was* one of the drier counties in England, but still…you never could tell what might happen when you lived on what amounted to an island. The morning Thelonious decided to drive out to the Broads gave every indication of being another perfect day and he was feeling on top of the world. Not only was he doing some of the best work he'd ever done in his career, but he hadn't so much as glimpsed DCI Sidebottom since that market-day Sunday in Kelton Market. Now that Thelonious knew the inspector lived quite some distance away from Little Acre, he felt as if a weight had been lifted from his shoulders. If Mrs. Baxter hadn't mentioned him the other night, he might have put him out of his mind altogether.

With it being a Monday, Thelonious didn't expect the boat hire people to be busy. On the contrary, they'd probably be thrilled to have some business and might even be more helpful when it came to accommodating him with extra cushions and such. Therefore he was stunned by the number of cars there ahead of him, not to mention the number of people milling about on the quay over where the hire boats were moored. It looked like a typical Saturday in August, not the early days of summer before the school holidays had begun. If this was the queue for boats, Thelonious didn't hold out much hope for getting one. He wanted to kick himself for not having booked in advance. Now he'd need to waste valuable time trying to find another facility to rent a boat from—and the one he was at now was the biggest and supposedly the best in the Broads.

There didn't seem to be any point in hanging about, since there wasn't anything interesting to photograph. It was essentially a car park with the boat hire place at one end and a cheap and nasty café with picnic tables set beneath a corrugated metal roof at the other. Whatever was worth seeing had to be seen from a boat. As Thelonious decided to cut his losses and return to the car, he heard the sound of a woman sobbing—and it was coming from the crowd gathered by the water. Although he could understand her disappointment on being told there were no more boats available for hire, he didn't think it was worth getting this upset about. When the sobbing turned to wailing, however, his concern got the better of him and he toddled over toward the quay to investigate. Perhaps someone had fallen into the water or even drowned. It probably happened more times than the tourist authority cared to admit. He'd better be careful himself, since he didn't fancy being fished out of Stanton Broad.

Suddenly a woman broke away from the crowd. She staggered a few feet, then doubled over, dropping to her knees. Her sobs and wails had become so loud that the patrons at the café abandoned their tables to see what was going on. Another woman rushed over to her side. Placing an arm around the distraught woman's shoulders, she led her away toward the boat hire office. Something was definitely up, thought Thelonious, and it wasn't good.

Just how not good it was became apparent when he noticed the police constables standing among the crowd.

Evidently he'd been correct and someone *had* drowned. "Please clear the area!" shouted one of the PCs in an attempt to disperse the spectators whose number had swelled since the arrival of those from the café. The crowd slowly began to thin out, bringing into view a large black sack made of vinyl or plastic lying on the quay's wood planking. A man dressed all in white was poised on one knee before it. Thelonious had seen enough police detective shows on television to know what a body bag looked like. No wonder the poor woman had come unhinged, especially if she'd had to identify whoever it was inside.

Not wanting to be a Peeping Tom to someone else's misery, Thelonious began to make his way back to the Mini. Framed in the plate-glass window of the boat hire office was the woman and her female companion, both of whom had gone inside and were now being handed cups of tea by an employee. Thelonious felt terrible for the poor woman, but there was nothing he could do. As he turned away from the scene, he heard a familiar voice calling out to him—and it belonged to the last person on earth he wanted to see.

Detective Chief Inspector Horatio Sidebottom came huffing through the car park from the direction of the quay, his farmer's face as red as a Rhesus monkey's backside. He looked even more out of shape than the last time Thelonious had set eyes on him—and that was really saying something. The man could've been on an NHS warning poster depicting a potential heart attack victim.

"Hang on a minute, Ted!" shouted the inspector.

Thelonious was only feet away from the Mini, his key already in paw. He could almost feel it turning in the ignition and hear the engine coming to life. He felt like an escaped prisoner getting caught by the guards as he was about to crawl through the hole he'd cut in the prison fence.

Sidebottom barrelled toward him like a lorry whose brakes had failed. Thelonious jumped out of the way for fear the inspector would collide with him and knock him to the pavement. "Thought that was yew!" wheezed the DCI, coming to a clumsy halt. Using the cuff of his sleeve, he swiped at the perspiration that had formed on his brow. His balding pate was likewise dotted with moisture and Thelonious resisted the urge to tell him he'd missed a spot.

"Phew!" Sidebottom placed his palm flat against his chest as if to calm his racing heartbeat. "Don't think I'll be taking up jogging any time soon!" he said with a self-deprecatory laugh. "Yew a jogger, Ted? Bet yew can run pretty fast with them little legs, eh?"

Visions of himself ripping out a chunk of the inspector's not-so-little leg filled Thelonious's head. Surely the DCI's remark constituted racism. Or maybe it was species-ism. Whatever it was, he didn't like it. Maybe it was time to file a complaint with Norfolk Constabulary. Their buffoon of a policeman had been harassing him ever since the first day he'd stepped foot in the county—and enough was enough!

"Terrible business, this," said Sidebottom, glancing back toward the quay. A police van had since pulled up alongside it and two men were busily loading the black bag into the back under the supervision of the man in white. He shook his head sadly. "We don't get murders round these parts."

"*Murder?*" Thelonious managed to croak, feeling the gastric stirrings of Mrs. Baxter's tinned beans in his belly.

"Old Augustus Stiffkey," replied the inspector, his expression suitably sombre. "Local publican. Family's been in these parts since Lord Nelson."

Thelonious couldn't for the life of him imagine what possible relevance a flatulent old dachshund in Little Acre would have to the Stiffkey family, other than perhaps having driven them out of town due to his digestive effluvium. Although Thelonious had been in the county long enough to pick up on the various eccentricities of the locals, relocating to escape from a farting dog sounded a bit much even for Norfolk standards. Then he realised that Sidebottom wasn't referring to The Drowned Duck's mangy mascot, but to Lord Admiral Horatio Nelson, the famous naval commander from Norfolk. That explained a lot. In fact, it likely went some way toward explaining DCI Sidebottom's rather uncommon Christian name of Horatio.

The inspector stared hard at Thelonious. "Yew been to Lower Forge, I take it?"

"Lower Forge?" Thelonious realised he sounded stupid, but he had no idea what the man was on about. He gazed longingly at his Mini, wishing he'd been quicker in his decision to leave. Had he simply turned around and driven back out of the car park when he'd first noticed the crowd of people on the quay, he could've avoided DCI Sidebottom altogether and would instead be on a boat a few miles away taking photos of the watery landscape and enjoying his day.

"Old Stiffkey knew how to run a pub, that's a fact," continued the inspector. "Been going to Ye Olde Father since I was a lad." He sighed heavily. "End of an era."

From what Thelonious managed to piece together from Sidebottom's random commentary, Ye Old Father was the name of the pub owned by the apparently now-deceased Augustus Stiffkey, whom he gathered was the occupant of the body bag. Said pub was located in the village of Lower Forge, which Thelonious recalled from a road sign was a mile or two down the road. It was beginning to make sense. It was also beginning to make sense that the DCI was once again trying to create a link between Thelonious and the murder of yet another publican in Norfolk.

"But I've never even been to Lower Forge!" he protested before the inspector could say anything further.

The DCI's eyes narrowed with suspicion. "How's that?"

Suddenly Thelonious couldn't speak. A giant hand gripped him by the throat and was squeezing until it had squeezed out all of the air—and the hand was attached to DCI Sidebottom's arm. Or at least it would've been had the man not been standing with his arms down at his sides as he studied Thelonious.

"Yew all right there, Ted? You're coming over a bit peaky."

Thelonious felt dizzy. Maybe it was because he hadn't

eaten much that morning, other than picking at some of Mrs. Baxter's tinned beans and washing them down with a cup of her tinny-tasting tea. The greasy smell of frying chips wafted over to him from the café, forcing a sound to surge up from his constricted gullet that was somewhere between a groan and a growl. Sidebottom continued to observe him closely, his farmer's face no longer in friendly mode. Rather than meeting his gaze, Thelonious stared down at his feet, wondering if he should wrap things up and get out of Norfolk before anything else happened. The county appeared to be a bigger hotbed for murder than Midsomer.

No doubt about it, Norfolk's answer to Lieutenant Columbo was in desperate need of a murder suspect—and Thelonious had been unlucky enough to have attracted his attention. The signs were all here, telling him to leave before it was too late. Maybe he should listen. As these thoughts ran through Thelonious's mind, he noticed a splodge of something liquid on the toe of his left trainer. He was certain it was honey. Its presence reminded him of the beekeeper from The Drowned Duck, which in turn reminded him of Fag-stain Man and Zimmer-frame Granny and Lord Nelson and Norfolk ale and lovely peanut-brittle cottages with To Let signs in front of them.

A surge of determination moved from Thelonious's honey-coated trainer to his deerstalker-hatted head. For the first time in his life he was beginning to feel as if he belonged somewhere and could be part of a community rather than always being removed from one. The residents of Little Acre were coming to accept him and treat him as one of their own. He'd be damned if he let some backwoods policeman run him out of the county. Why, he had just as much right to be here as anyone!

Sidebottom's eyebrows quirked upward, as if trying to fill in the gap between them and his receding hairline as he waited for an explanation—if not a confession. Well, Thelonious had nothing to confess. Instead he trundled resolutely over to his Mini, all but daring the inspector to stop him, unlocked the door, and levered himself up onto the driver's seat in record time.

"Maybe you should speak to Mrs. Baxter about those four men she has staying there," said Thelonious, deciding it was high time to state the obvious. Even if they had nothing to do with the murders, he was willing to bet they had something to do with *something*. Gunning the engine, Thelonious jerked the gear into reverse and shot out from between the neighbouring vehicles. He floored it out of the car park, nearly sideswiping a black Audi that had just pulled in.

Chapter Fifteen

DESMOND REFUSED TO LEAVE THE HOUSE. He didn't go food shopping, he didn't go to the off-licence, and he didn't go down the pub. He claimed he had a bad case of the trots and couldn't be away from the toilet—a malady his brother immediately blamed on the ready-meals they'd been eating. Fortunately the Clarks still had a good enough supply of them on hand, since Vinnie wouldn't go food shopping either. That had always been Desmond's job, as were most things domestic in the Clark household. Vinnie had no issue with trips to the off-licence, however. If they ran out of food, they'd have enough lager to keep them alive until Boxing Day.

It wasn't a lie that Desmond was suffering, but it wasn't on account of anything he'd eaten. He was worried—worried and scared. Morning, afternoon and night he stayed glued to the television news, shitting himself as he waited for reports of a bloodied tyre iron being found in a Cambridgeshire river—or rather on a boat in a Cambridgeshire river. He surfed every station he could find, including the 24-hour news channel, even going downstairs into the lounge in the middle of the night to switch the telly back on. He'd also added *Crimewatch* to his viewing list, since there was always a chance the weapon would be mentioned as local authorities reached out to the public for leads. The coppers caught a lot of dodgy geezers thanks to that programme—Desmond hoped he wouldn't end up becoming one of them. Because any trail of breadcrumbs leading to Vinnie Clark would likewise lead to himself. Hard to believe no one had turned it in yet, especially the person whose punt it had fallen into…unless maybe he'd missed the report on the news and the thing was already being examined for forensic evidence. Not knowing was driving him mental, and he didn't know how much more he could take.

Not surprisingly, Desmond's choice in TV programming didn't sit too well with his brother, whose viewing preferences consisted entirely of sports and porn. "Oi, bruv, if I didn't know no better, I'd think ya fancied that Welsh geezer from off the telly!" he'd said to Desmond on more than one occasion, referring to a male news presenter on BBC One's evening broadcast.

Desmond reckoned it was better for Vinnie to think he'd turned into a raging poofter than to know the *real* reason why he was suddenly so obsessed with the news. Maybe he'd start listening to some of them boy bands while he was at it. Might as well let his brother take him for a complete bender. Desmond's supposed conversion to homosexuality could well be his ticket out of here. Vinnie would probably hand over the entire takings from the Broads job just to be shot of him! Having a gay brother wouldn't be in keeping with Vinnie Clark's tough masculine image. If Desmond hadn't been so busy shitting himself over the tyre iron, he'd be busting a gut laughing.

Vinnie was getting careless—careless and big-headed. He'd started splashing the cash about again too, especially on them local bints who couldn't keep their big fat gobs shut unless it was to put some bloke's knob in it—in this case, *Vinnie's*. Seemed like every morning when Desmond went downstairs into the kitchen to make himself a cuppa there'd be some stroppy minger sitting at the table drinking the Clarks' tea and eating their toast and using up all their orange marmalade. And it wasn't just the one either. It was like musical chairs with a different bird every day, each stupider than the last. Where'd his brother find them? Desmond reckoned that they must've come from their local. That shithole of a boozer was a magnet for every council estate chav in the neighbourhood, especially them single mums who'd got themselves up the duff by their sixteenth birthday, entitling them to hop aboard the housing and benefits express. One of Vinnie's slappers had even brought along her sprog. Desmond had found the kid plonked down in front of the telly watching Vinnie's favourite porn channel while Vinnie and his bit of skirt were at it upstairs. Crikey.

The fact they'd dumped the latest geezer's body in one of the Broads marked a big change in what his brother referred to as their "modus operandi," which added even more to Desmond's anxiety. "Ain't no challenge in just offin' the geezer and leavin' him in the pub till somebody trips over him! Let's shake things up a bit!" were Vinnie's words. By "shaking things up," he meant deviating from their usual plan of making it look like the publican had been robbed, then beaten to death as an afterthought. He'd said it would confuse the coppers—and for Vinnie, anything that made a copper's life more difficult was worth the extra time and effort and, in this case, *risk*. By moving the body to another location and dumping it, Vinnie had also managed to squeeze some extra dosh out of the posh bloke who'd ordered the hit, since additional risks meant additional fees in the brothers' line of work. Whether Desmond would get his hands on any of this extra money—or any money at all—remained to be seen. Maybe he'd never make it to the Costa Brava. Maybe he'd end up being sent down. And it wouldn't be like the last time either. He'd be in with the big leagues, locked up with *real* murderers—hard-core geezers who'd have him bending over to touch his toes before anyone could say "Bob's your uncle!"

As Desmond became increasingly more depressed about the inescapability of his fate and the collapse of his plans in the Costa Brava, Vinnie went in the opposite direction, bouncing off the walls like he was beaked up on something, though Desmond hadn't been able to find any evidence of drugs in the house other than a blister packet of paracetamol six months past its sell-by date. "I tell ya, we're goin' places, bruv!" was Vinnie's current catch phrase, indicating to Desmond that he was planning to build some big empire with the Clark brothers as hit men to London's celebrity elite. Seemed to Desmond that the only way out of this crazy situation was if he got banged up again—and if that happened, he'd be inside for a very long time.

So Desmond watched the news and waited, wondering how long it would be before the Old Bill showed up at the front door.

Chapter Sixteen

"YEW GET ONE PHONE CALL."

Thelonious perched on an uncomfortable plastic chair located somewhere within the bowels of the headquarters for Norfolk CID, his short legs dangling into space. Although he'd already been given the whole caution routine, DCI Sidebottom continued to stare expectantly at him, no doubt anticipating a full confession, after which everyone could have a cup of tea and go home—well, at least everyone but the poor blighter who'd been arrested. The inspector seemed to sense that Thelonious had no one to call, no one to come to his rescue. Maybe that was why he'd been such an easy target for an incompetent policeman in search of a scapegoat.

The fact that Thelonious didn't possess the physical capability to hoist the dead body of a fully grown adult male into the boot of his Mini Cooper, then pull it back out again, either carrying or dragging it to the quay to dump into Stanton Broad didn't come into play. Why, he had enough trouble dealing with a suitcase! But in the inspector's eyes, he was guilty, full stop. Thank goodness Britain had abolished hanging or Thelonious's neck would be getting fitted for a bespoke noose.

The office he'd been taken to reeked of onions. Judging by its overall untidiness as well as the framed desk photo of a frumpy woman resembling the one he'd seen looking at flower pots the Sunday he'd run into the inspector at Kelton Market, Thelonious concluded that he must be in DCI Sidebottom's personal lair. A tin of Coke along with a half-eaten sandwich lay forgotten on a food-stained desk blotter; this must've been the source of the smell. Although no fan of raw onions, Thelonious's belly began to rumble. How he could be hungry at a time like this he couldn't imagine, yet hungry he was. Even Mrs. Baxter's tinned beans would have been a treat right about now. At least then Thelonious might've been given the satisfaction of rewarding the DCI's olfactory senses with a few potent farts that would have made Lord Nelson envious.

"Did you speak to those four men?" demanded Thelonious, not holding out much hope for an affirmative answer.

"And what men might yew be referring to, Ted?"

"The men staying at Mrs. Baxter's!" he roared. He'd had enough of this nonsense. If Sidebottom couldn't see what was staring him in the face, then Thelonious hadn't a hope in hell of feeling the Norfolk sunshine on his fur again.

The inspector shook his big head and smiled indulgently. "Now Ted, surely yew can do better than that?"

Thelonious should never have returned to Wickham Marsh. It was like returning to the scene of the crime—and yet it hadn't even been his crime to commit. All he'd done was go to the village so that he could view that adorable little peanut-brittle cottage he'd seen for rent. He'd booked an appointment with the letting agent, practically crowing over the phone on being told it was still available—*and* at a rent a damned sight less than what he'd been paying in London.

The next morning he was on his way back to the Fens, planning how he'd decorate the place before he'd even taken a look inside.

Excited about his new life in Norfolk, Thelonious left Little Acre two hours earlier than he'd needed to. Despite being told his viewing was the first scheduled for that morning, he dared not risk being gazumped by the next person in the queue in the event he didn't arrive on time. He had no idea how competitive the rental market might be in the area. In London a good property, especially one going for a good price, would be gone in the blink of an eye. Thelonious didn't want to end up being late due to an overturned tractor or spilled bales of hay or any other Norfolk mode of mishap that might happen on the road. He wanted that cottage—and nothing was going to stop him from having it!

As it turned out, he still got to Wickham Marsh two hours ahead of schedule, only to discover that the estate agent's office wouldn't be open for another hour yet. Since he had time to kill, he decided to have a wander on what he hoped would soon be his local high street. Thelonious was surprised that the arts and crafts gallery was open and ready for business this early, so he toddled on in, thinking he'd check out what was on offer. Perhaps he might find something suitable for his new digs. If he was going to be living in the village, then he should help support the local artisans' community. He might even do something with a few of the photos he'd been taking. He didn't need to turn *all* of them over to his publisher—there were plenty to go around. Who knows, he could try selling his work through the gallery.

With this in mind, Thelonious asked for a business card from the girl working there, ignoring her rude gawping. The locals would get used to him soon enough, just as they had in Little Acre. Speaking of which, once he'd moved here he could always pop over to The Drowned Duck in case he missed the place; it wouldn't be that far of a drive. Or perhaps he'd find another pub—one with plenty of Norfolk character, not to mention plenty of Norfolk ale.

As Thelonious mapped out his wonderful new life in Wickham Marsh, he suddenly found himself standing in front of The Fat Badger. Although it hadn't been intentional, the place was difficult to avoid what with it being smack in the middle of the high street. Through the mullioned front window lay a rubble-strewn interior representing the chaos of a major renovation project. The pub was being gutted from floor to ceiling. Thelonious could see a haze of dust hanging in the air like smog; he shuddered to think of the toxic pollutants that might be floating about in there. The scene saddened him. It looked as if someone were trying to erase history and, along with it, the memories of those who'd drunk their pints here as well as those who'd pulled them.

A breeze blew in from the fen, triggering a rustling sound above Thelonious's head. He glanced up to see a banner festooned across the façade of The Fat Badger. It moved determinedly, as if demanding to call attention to itself.

OPENING SOON!
THE CROWN OF WICKHAM
A PAOLO LOUIS BLACK PUB

Beneath the banner the old wooden sign for The Fat Badger hung stubbornly from its hinges, proclaiming the pub's previous identity. Thelonious knew it was a matter of time before that too, would be gone. How many more pubs did this Black character need? If this was London maybe he could understand it. But Norfolk? And what village would be the next to fall to this pub-slayer's sword, Little Acre? Try as he might, Thelonious couldn't envision the beekeeper or Zimmer-frame Granny having a natter at the bar of some snooty gastropub. Nor could he envision Fag-stain Man, despite being the most famous rock guitarist on the planet, gulping down his favourite whisky under the watchful eye of some snooty barmaid. There'd definitely be plenty of lively conversation tonight at The Drowned Duck when he told everyone the news!

Thelonious had to admit that his keenness to become a resident of Wickham Marsh had dulled a bit thanks to the looming presence of yet another of Paolo Louis Black's overpriced and overhyped pubs. But apparently there were enough mugs around willing to spend a fortune on a burger that wouldn't fill the belly of a sparrow. Well, Paolo Louis Black would be waiting a long time before he'd be dipping his greedy fingers in Thelonious's pocket again.

Since he had less than ten minutes remaining until his appointment, Thelonious decided to head over to the letting agent's. Maybe they'd open up early if they saw him waiting outside the door. The staff, or at least some of them, had already arrived—he could see them milling about through the display window. Just as he was getting ready to cross the road to their office, a black Audi came speeding toward him from the bottom of the high street. Veering into the oncoming lane of traffic, it pulled up in front of The Fat Badger, parking illegally at the kerb.

The London parking permit on the vehicle's windscreen pinched like a burr in Thelonious's paw. He knew this car. In fact, he knew it very well. As he debated whether to give the driver a piece of his mind or continue on his way to his appointment, a middle-aged man with ginger hair got out from behind the steering wheel. Seemingly unconcerned that his expensive motor might be clamped for parking where it shouldn't be parked, he engaged the alarm and strode up to the pub's front door as if he owned the place.

Thelonious was certain he knew the man from somewhere. But before he could figure out from *where*, a familiar voice reached his ears, destroying the promise of a pleasant weekday morning.

"Ted!"

Thelonious contemplated throwing himself in front of a moving vehicle. A lorry might do the trick. Or better yet, why not throw the bane of his existence in front of it? Cursing himself for dawdling at the kerb instead of getting his furry backside over the road to the estate agent's, Thelonious acted as if he hadn't heard the greeting. He was far more concerned with the fact that the "closed" sign on the door had been flipped to "open." A customer was already inside the office, speaking to a woman at one of the desks. This had to be the next appointment for the cottage. Just as he'd feared, he was about to be gazumped.

DCI Sidebottom appeared at Thelonious' side, his farmer's face wearing its characteristic heart-attack pink. "Take it yew saw Paolo Louis Black," he said, indicating the Audi parked at the kerb flouting the law. "Guess he'll be putting Wickham Marsh on the map soon."

So the ginger-haired prat driving the black Audi was none other than the celebrity chef whose goal was to singlehandedly destroy every decent pub in Britain. It all made sense now. The only thing that *didn't* make sense was why the inspector still felt it his right to continue pestering Thelonious by detaining him in the middle of Wickham Marsh high street. Surely Sidebottom should've wrapped things up in the village if Black had already laid claim to The Fat Badger. If there was any more evidence to be found, the demolition job currently in progress would've put paid to it.

Thelonious gazed miserably at the estate agent's office. The woman who'd been at her desk chatting with the customer was now in the process of removing a listing from the window display. He knew it was his peanut-brittle cottage. His new life in Wickham Marsh was disintegrating before his eyes and he wondered if he should just go ahead and kill Sidebottom and, while he was at it, Paolo Louis Black. Since the inspector already believed he was guilty of murder, he might as well go for broke.

"Where's your car parked, Ted?"

"My car?" It seemed like an odd question. Maybe he needed a lift somewhere, in which case it was pretty cheeky of him to expect Thelonious to provide one. Surely detective chief inspectors had their own vehicles—unless all those budgetary cutbacks were now forcing them to take public transport along with the rest of the hoi polloi. Well, Thelonious wasn't inclined to give Sidebottom a lift *anywhere*. Moreover, he wanted to ask the DCI why he wasn't doing something about Paolo Louis Black's illegally parked car instead of worrying about where he'd parked his, but he never got the chance. The inspector was already on his mobile phone, speaking to somebody about impounding a vehicle.

Thelonious felt like jumping up and down and cheering. For the first time he was actually beginning to have some respect for Sidebottom—at least the man wasn't allowing himself to be influenced by celebrity status. A law breaker was a law breaker. It shouldn't matter how much money he had or how popular he was on television or how many gastropubs he owned. Perhaps Thelonious would stick around to watch the fun when Paolo Louis Black's expensive black Audi got towed away from in front of his new gastropub.

Sidebottom concluded his conversation, returning the mobile to his inside jacket pocket. "I think yew'd best come with me, Ted," he said, reaching for Thelonious's arm.

It was at that moment when Thelonious realised it was *his* vehicle the inspector had been referring to in his phone call—his beloved Mini Cooper!

As he tried to wrench his arm out from DCI Sidebottom's surprisingly firm grip, a police squad car pulled up to the kerb behind Paolo Louis Black's illegally parked Audi. Two fresh-scrubbed young constables climbed out. Rather than ticketing and clamping the Audi, they marched directly up to Thelonious. Sidebottom's grip tightened on his arm as one of them began reading from a card.

Thelonious T. Bear, good citizen and hard-working British taxpayer, was under arrest.

Chapter Seventeen

Augustus Stiffkey.

Hearing the name said out loud and seeing his face filling the screen of the Clark's high-definition television really made it hit home for Desmond. The geezer had a wife, kids, grandkids—people who loved him and would miss him. And two brothers from Bow had taken it all away for the sake of a few quid. Okay, so maybe it was a lot more than a few quid—a few grand if anyone was counting, but still....

Hell, maybe he was developing a conscience in his old age. Or maybe he was tired. Whatever the case, the buzz just wasn't there anymore. It hadn't been there for a long time. He felt sick and empty.

So when Stiffkey's missus came on the telly all weepy and begging for someone to please come forward to help with the inquiry into his murder, Desmond nearly lost it right there and had to run upstairs to the toilet before he hurled all over the sofa. He still didn't get why nobody had mentioned the tyre iron. Either it hadn't been found or the coppers were keeping back the information till things were further along in the investigation. Coppers. They did that sometimes.

When he returned to the lounge, *Crimewatch* had been replaced by a pair of underage-looking females rogering each other with battery-operated gadgets that looked like what the demolition men used to break up pavement. "Oi! Can ya believe the size of that thing?" cried Vinnie, having confiscated Desmond's place on the sofa. He was in the midst of clipping his toenails. Yellowed half-moons of what resembled bits of rotting animal hoof littered the carpet and sofa, making Desmond want to hurl again. "That bird's twat is so big London transport could run the District line through it! Blimey!" Vinnie pounded his fist on the arm of the sofa, releasing into the air at least five years' worth of dust. "She's gonna have a right echo in there by the time that blonde bird's done with 'er!"

As his brother continued to shout and pummel the sofa, Desmond fled into the kitchen and made himself a cup of tea. He switched on the radio in an attempt to drown out Vinnie's raging testosterone and the exaggerated female moans coming from the TV speakers, then began to bang his shaved head against the edge of the sink until it felt as if the impact had loosened his back teeth. No doubt about it—he was reaching the end of his tether. He was either going to crack or he was going to do something there'd be no coming back from.

"Oi!" yelled Vinnie. "Make me a brew while you're at it, bruv!"

His brother's voice had the effect of someone setting fire to his balls. Vinnie treated him like a skivvy and had done for years. Question is, why'd he put up with it for so long? Refilling the kettle with water from the tap, Desmond slammed it back onto the heating plate. He set about preparing a second mug with milk and two sugars, recycling his used teabag instead of using a fresh one. As he waited for the water to boil, he found himself wishing there was some rat poison in the house. A little sprinkle in Vinnie's tea and—.

He wondered if he could do it—actually kill his own brother. Easy to think about, but putting it into practice was another matter. Still, offing Vinnie sounded like a great way to get shot of all his problems—the biggest one being Vinnie. For the first time in weeks Desmond felt himself smile and he began to whistle along to the cheesy ABBA tune playing on the radio.

"Cheers, bruv," said Vinnie when Desmond brought him in his mug of tea. The fact that it was weak as dishwater went unnoticed, since Vinnie had more important things to occupy his attention—namely the appearance of two additional pieces of jailbait on the telly. "Des, me old son, ya really missed some action! That blonde bird—"

Desmond planted himself on what small amount of space remained of the sofa that wasn't taken up with his brother or his toenail clippings. "We really need to talk, Vin."

Vinnie dragged his eyes off the TV screen to gape in disbelief at his brother. *"Talk?* What's so important it can't wait? Can't ya see I'm watchin' a film? Ya want me to lose track of the plot or what?"

As far as Desmond could tell, the only plot seemed to be these bints' desire to cause serious physical damage to each other. Though he enjoyed a bit of porn as much as the next bloke, his tastes didn't run to the freak show variety. Film or no film, he wasn't about to let his brother off so easily. "Vinnie, we gotta talk about sortin' the money."

Vinnie's face went stony. Desmond knew that look—it was the same look Vinnie always got right before he went psycho on you. "Money? *What* money?"

"The money from them Norfolk jobs. It's time to divvy up." Desmond was bricking it, but he'd be damned if he let his brother know. He wanted his share of the dosh—and he wanted it *now*. He didn't even care anymore about the takings from their other jobs. What they'd pulled in from Norfolk would be plenty good to get him started in the Costa Brava, though he'd still need to pick up some extra income to keep himself going, like lifting wallets from sunburned British tourists and such. Since that sort of thing was always blamed on the local pond scum, he wasn't likely to take the rap for it.

"So what's the big rush all of a sudden?" Vinnie asked suspiciously, no longer concerned about missing any of the intricate plotline of his film. "Don't ya trust me? Ya think I'm gonna go runnin' off to the Costa Brava with all the dosh?" From the creepy look he was giving Desmond, it was like Vinnie had him sussed from day one.

Desmond's lips felt glued shut. He knew he should say something so as not to appear guilty, but he couldn't get his mouth to open. He'd been so careful. He'd written nothing down—it was all inside his head or saved in his email account online. No effing way could Vinnie have cottoned on to his escape plan—not unless he'd gone down the library, logged onto a computer and hacked into his email. And the idea of Vinnie stepping foot in a public library or using a computer was about as likely as those three geezers in Norfolk returning from the grave to open up a pub together.

As if to needle him, Vinnie said: "Whassup, bruv? Nothin' else to say? Seemed like ya had plenty to say a minute ago."

Desmond stared at the television screen. Anything was better than having to look his brother in the eye—because if he did, Vinnie would know everything. Though he probably already did, those remarks about the Costa Brava hitting too close to the bone to be random. It had all been for nothing. Desmond should've walked out ages ago instead of sticking around waiting for a pay-out that would never come. Now he was an accomplice in three murders—cold-blooded premeditated murders. There was no wrapping up what they'd done in cotton wool or sticking a pink satin ribbon on it. There was no turning back the clock and giving those geezers back their lives. Three men were dead. And Desmond had blood on his hands even though he hadn't done the killing.

The fact they'd been hired to do it didn't make a bit of

difference. It would be the word of two ex-cons from Bow against the word of a famous chef from off the telly—the same famous chef who'd gone to Buckingham Palace, along with a BBC camera crew, to prepare a big birthday dinner for the Queen and her special guests. Vinnie and Desmond Clark would be a right pair of laughing stocks if they tried to tell such a tale. A jury would take them for a couple of blood-thirsty hoods hunting for some easy pickings in the Norfolk countryside. Not only would the Clarks get sent down for the rest of their lives, they'd become the poster boys for the movement to reinstate hanging in Britain.

Vinnie jumped up from the sofa, sending half-moons of toenail sailing through the air like yellow confetti. "I'm goin' down the pub. Don't much like the smell in 'ere." A moment later Desmond heard the front door slam.

He ran over to the front window to watch as Vinnie sauntered down the road in the direction of the high street, his shaved head shining in the streetlamp as he passed beneath it until he disappeared from view. From as far back as Desmond could remember his brother had that cocksure swagger. Funny how something as simple as a walk could tell you about a person's background and history. In Vinnie's case, it said he was an East End geezer through and through. There could be no mistaking him for anything else.

It had now become a matter of survival—it was either him or Vinnie. He knew what his brother would do if he were in his shoes, and he wouldn't think twice about it either. Desmond went over to the phone, sucking in a deep breath as he dialled the Crimestoppers number that had been shown on *Crimewatch* earlier that evening.

He had an anonymous tip for them.

Chapter Eighteen

A KEY CLANGED IN THE LOCK OF THE holding cell. "Right, you're free to go," said a young pink-eared police constable, his tone indicating that he didn't care one way or the other if the prisoner was set free or left to rot. The door swung open and the PC stood there gawping as Thelonious hopped down from the bench, snapping chewing gum between teeth that looked as if they'd been subjected to one too many sweets. Had Thelonious not been on the wrong side of the cell door, he might've asked the lad if he'd ever heard of a toothbrush. Why, he'd seen cleaner choppers on his foraging cousins that lived in the wild!

His short legs felt unsteady beneath him, and he stopped for a moment to rub his backside with the pads of his paws, trying to ease the discomfort from having to sit for so long on a hard surface. That bench hadn't exactly been the last word in comfort, though Thelonious supposed it was better than sitting on a dirty floor. The cell didn't look as if it had been cleaned within the last year and it was probably exposed to a lot of turnover, considering the eagerness of certain Norfolk police inspectors to lock up innocent members of the public.

Thelonious had lost track of time. Had he been here an hour? A day? A week? No, it couldn't have been a week—he would be dead of starvation by now if it had been that long. One thing was certain: he hadn't been given any food. He hadn't even been given a cup of tea. Surely there were provisions in place that prohibited the police from starving their prisoners to death. If he'd been locked up for more than a few hours, they would have brought him something to eat and drink by now. The fact that they had not appeared to indicate he'd only been here a matter of hours.

Nevertheless, it had felt like forever to Thelonious. He shuddered to think what it must be like being locked up for years—the endless days stretching into endless months, then endless years, until finally your sentence, if not your life, was over. He envisioned himself dressed in prison garb several sizes too large, lying on a smelly bunk whiling away the time playing mournful songs on a battered old harmonica. He'd probably watched too many of those old black-and-white American prison films, but the boredom of the situation was no doubt accurate. For however many hours he'd been inside the holding cell Thelonious had nothing to occupy his time—not unless watching the CCTV camera that was watching him watching it could be considered an occupation. Even the sanest of individuals would go crazy in these circumstances, not to mention his own kind, for whom being caged up signified *the end*.

He expected an explanation, an apology—at least *something* to indicate that this had been one huge mistake. Instead Thelonious had to run like mad to keep up with the quick strides of the constable's long legs. Whatever information he needed, he clearly wasn't going to get from this kid. He reckoned the big apology would be coming from DCI Sidebottom, and he expected to be taken into the inspector's onion-scented office, where the man himself would be waiting for him with a cup of tea, wearing a suitable expression of *mea culpa*. Thelonious would have some very choice words for him, too. He wasn't about to let this trumped-up policeman off the hook with a weak smile and an even weaker cup of builder's tea.

Instead Thelonious found himself in another part of the station signing for his personal belongings. Sidebottom still hadn't put in an appearance, but by then he was so grateful to discover that his camera bag hadn't been tampered with and all his equipment was present and accounted for that he didn't want to make a fuss, gift horses and all that. The fact that the police had confiscated his deerstalker hat when he'd been brought in was yet another humiliation Thelonious had been forced to endure, and he returned it to its rightful place on his furry head, tugging it down over his ears and feeling more like his old self again.

As for why he'd been arrested in the first place and was suddenly being set free, no one would tell him anything. Pink Ears had vanished, and the sullen fellow returning his things to him simply glared, seeming put out by even having to deal with him at all. Thelonious could only conclude that someone whose authority overrode that of DCI Sidebottom's had enough common sense to realise that he had nothing to do with these local killings. To imagine for a minute that he could have bludgeoned to death three grown men—men three times his size and even more times his weight—was preposterous. Undoubtedly the inspector was too ashamed to show his face and had gone into hiding. Or else he'd been fired.

Thelonious hoped it was the latter.

Fortunately the Mini Cooper had avoided being ripped apart in a search for evidence that didn't exist. Aside from a scratch on the driver's-side door that hadn't been there previously, everything appeared to be normal. Thelonious had to pay a fee before the impound facility would release the vehicle. When he brought up about the scratch, he was shown the inventory form, which conveniently indicated its presence from when the car was first brought in. It was Thelonious's word against the Biblical weight of the inventory form—and he knew who'd win that argument.

Despite the inconvenience he'd been put through, no offers had been forthcoming at the police station to give Thelonious a lift to collect his car, so he'd had to pay for a taxi. Adding in the extortionate impound fees and a potential re-spray bill for the car door, this fiasco was costing him a small fortune—and it was thanks to some backwater Lieutenant Columbo with all the investigative skills of a wet kitchen sponge. Maybe it was just as well Sidebottom *hadn't* put in an appearance, because Thelonious might have gnawed both of the man's legs off instead of just one.

By the time he got back to Baxter House it was nightfall. He found the place in a state of chaos, with a hysterical Mrs. Baxter going in circles in the entry hall like a dog chasing its own tail. Her every word was a blubbering wail that made Thelonious long for the peace and tranquillity of the holding cell he'd been occupying a few hours ago. It took him several minutes to make sense of what she was on about—and when he did, he wasn't particularly surprised. According to the landlady, the three Belgians and their Russian comrade had effectively done a runner, leaving unpaid the previous week's room tariff. Since they'd been guests for several weeks—nearly the same length of time as Thelonious—Mrs. Baxter didn't think it necessary to take an imprint of their credit card, relying instead on the fact that they'd always paid in cash at the end of each week's stay. Thelonious suspected she preferred this paperless trail, likely pocketing the money rather than reporting it to the Inland Revenue as income from the business. Having consistently paid his fair share of income tax, he didn't have much sympathy for her plight.

The four men had been in such a hurry to leave that they hadn't bothered to take their clothes or other personal items. Thelonious reckoned they were probably on a ferry to mainland Europe by now and was about to ask Mrs. Baxter if she'd rung the police, then clamped his jaw shut. The thought of coming face to face with any more of Norfolk's finest was enough to make his fur fall out. Besides which, if this swift departure had anything to do with the business of the murdered publicans—and considering the quartet's dodgy behaviour this wasn't beyond the realm of possibility—Thelonious didn't want to be linked to the crimes any more than he already was. He'd only just got *out* of a jail cell—he didn't want to go back inside one!

"And they were such charming gentlemen, too!" howled Mrs. Baxter, wiping her streaming nose on the flower-patterned sleeve of her housedress. "That Igor was always so complimentary of my breakfasts! Why, just the other morning—"

"*Charming?*" echoed a voice that sounded as if it were trying to force its way out from beneath the ground. "You call this '*charming*?'"

A garden gnome come to life clomped into the entry hall, a trail of lawn detritus following in his wake. He was carrying a heap of dirty washing, and he dropped it onto the carpet with a disgusted scowl. "Stinks like something died in there."

"Mr. Bear, I believe you haven't had the pleasure of meeting my husband," said Mrs. Baxter, sniffing.

Pleasure wasn't quite the word Thelonious had in mind now that he was finally up close and personal with the man of mystery himself. No wonder Mr. Baxter had been keeping a low profile—any prospective guests catching a glimpse of the fellow would've been off in a flash. It certainly went some way toward explaining why business was down at the B&B. Not knowing what else to do, Thelonious stuck out his paw for a handshake. It went ignored.

"That room's going to want fumigating," Mr. Baxter informed his wife, though he was looking at Thelonious when he said it.

Thelonious wasn't sure whether to take offence or excuse the landlady's husband for being distracted with the trials and tribulations of running a bed and breakfast, especially one where the guests ran off without paying their bill. Embarrassed, he dropped his paw back down to his side.

"*Charming?*" Mr. Baxter repeated, his already uncomely features twisting in a particularly nasty sneer. "If they were so *charming*, then why'd your boyfriend Sidebottom show up here looking for them?"

The garden gnome turned on a grass-caked heel and exited the room, leaving Thelonious alone with his wife and the pile of reeking clothes. Among the disarray of fabric on the floor was a pair of Y-fronts in serious need of being set fire to, its condition no doubt inspired by one of Baxter House's renowned breakfasts. Thelonious was willing to bet the undergarment had belonged to the "charming" Igor.

Flustered by her spouse's rude departure, the landlady's round face turned a bright shade of pink. "You must excuse my husband, Mr. Bear. He gets easily upset."

If I looked like that, I'd get easily upset too, Thelonious wanted to say. Instead he just nodded. As he turned in the direction of the stairs, Mrs. Baxter suddenly grabbed his paw and burst into tears. "Oh, Mr. Bear! I'm so unhappy!" The waterworks had been switched to full power now and Thelonious wavered between making a run for his room or the car park. No wonder those four oddballs had left without taking their kit. If he had any sense, he'd do the same.

"I should never have married that man!" sobbed the landlady. "But he was so handsome back then—you should've seen him!"

Thelonious couldn't imagine Mr. Baxter ever being handsome—unless maybe you had a thing for garden gnomes. Although he'd heard all the usual derogatory jokes about people from Norfolk, he'd yet to hear anything about the local women becoming romantically involved with garden statuary.

"And I was such a pretty little thing, too!"

This too, Thelonious found hard to swallow, particularly the "little" part. Mrs. Baxter's reminiscence for the romantic days of yore was causing the fur on the back of his neck to stand up—a warning sign that had never yet failed to be wrong.

"I'm sure *you* know how to treat a woman, Mr. Bear," she added, giving his paw a meaningful squeeze.

The statement hung in the air between them. The terror those few words struck in Thelonious's heart was worse than anything that had been going through his mind while locked inside the cell at the police station. Mrs. Baxter had a hungry look in her eyes and she began to bend down toward him, her lips pursing outward like a Venus flytrap about to catch its prey.

Wrenching his paw out of the landlady's claw-like grasp, Thelonious bolted for the stairs, his short legs moving at such speed his deerstalker hat nearly flew off his head. He reached his room without further mishap, locked the door and pulled a chair in front of it.

He hoped he'd survive the night.

Epilogue

DESMOND SIGHED WITH CONTENTMENT AS he reclined on a lounge chair facing the brilliant blue of the Mediterranean, drinking his sangria. The golden sand baked beneath the Catalonian sun, as did he—and he loved every minute of it. Bow was a world away with its grim tower blocks and graffiti and stabbings. So what if it was going upmarket? No effing way would he go back to that hell hole!

Not that he could. He'd be picked up the minute he landed at Stansted.

Desmond had covered his lounger with a Union Jack beach towel so the plastic slats wouldn't get too hot against his already sunburned skin. With any luck he might turn a nice shade of brown once all the peeling had stopped. He was on his third sangria of the afternoon bought from the poolside bar of a nearby hotel. He reckoned he was getting enough nutrition from the fruit to justify the number of times he kept ordering his current drink of choice, the beer being mostly shit in these parts. This was Desmond's favourite stretch of beach—it had the perfect mix of tourists and natives and was just a short walk from his little apartment. There were also lots of bars and restaurants nearby. He'd done good choosing this area.

While slathering another coat of factor 50 sunblock onto his chest and arms, he noticed a fit pair of English birds sashaying past, their sun-pinkened backsides on full display. The strings of their thong bikini bottoms wedged inside their bum cracks practically shouted at Desmond to pluck them out, and he felt a bit of action in the tackle department as he imagined himself doing so. A moment later a fit pair of Spanish birds went by in equally revealing swimwear, their backsides the shade of toffee. They always tanned better than the English birds, though Desmond didn't care whether it was pink or brown or even blue just so long as it was all out there. It was like watching a non-stop parade of tits and arse. Life couldn't get any sweeter!

Tonight after some tapas he'd go out on the pull at the local bars. There was always plenty of action, not to mention plenty of Sangria to get them foreign birds loosened up, the fruity plonk on offer well cheaper than what the better hotels charged. Desmond had found that out pretty quick and now made a point not to go chucking money about when he didn't need to. Of course, if a bird was paying that was different. He'd been surprised by how many weren't shy to get their purses out, especially the ones that liked to brag about their jobs back home like them London birds, who always seemed to work in marketing or PR. It was a man's world all right. The birds not only bought the drinks, but put it all on offer for free, practically sticking it in your face. A bloke didn't even need to ask for it.

After getting an eyeful of those pink arses, Desmond was in the mood to get some English tonight—"a full English" as he referred to it. Blimey, he sounded more like his brother all the time! One good thing about these English bints was that they weren't too fussed about the quality of their drinks, only that the drinks kept coming—as would Desmond after he went back with them to their rooms. He never took the tourist birds home to his place. Why bother when they had a posh hotel room with a maid to do the tidying up after they made a pig's mess of it? If he knew they were leaving the next day, he'd help himself to the legal tender in their handbags after he'd shot his load. He never worried about getting caught. They were always so bladdered on cheap plonk they probably didn't notice the loss until they were at the airport duty free buying more cheap plonk to take back home with them.

Desmond couldn't imagine ever leaving here. The Costa Brava was paradise. Vinnie would've loved it.

Unfortunately for Vinnie, sand and sea and tits and arse (at least those of the female variety) weren't on the menu at Belmarsh prison. Neither were tapas and sangria. That Crimestoppers number had worked a right treat, mused Desmond, chewing on a soggy grape he'd fished out of his glass of sangria. Guess his brother hadn't reckoned on the Old Bill nabbing him or else he'd have stored all that money someplace more secure, like in a safe-deposit box at the bank instead of under the mattress like some senile old bag who thought the War was still on. Poor Vinnie. Hopefully he wouldn't go dropping the soap in the shower!

While Desmond Clark was busy contemplating the pleasures to be had in the beautiful Costa Brava, Vinnie Clark was busy plotting ways to kill him once he got out of the toilet known as Belmarsh, if not before. He still couldn't believe his brother had stitched him up. Bad enough being a grass, but to sell your own flesh and blood down the river, your only family—that was just plain low. Well, he'd get what was coming to him. Vinnie'd see to that.

In the meantime he had enough shit to deal with. There were some right dodgy geezers in this joint—worse than any he'd ever come across—and he'd come across plenty. Funny thing was, the tougher and meaner they were, the more likely it was that they'd ram it up your jacksie when you weren't paying attention. So Vinnie had to be on his guard more than ever, meaning he needed to be an even tougher and meaner geezer than they were. It sure paid to have a few murders under your belt.

The boredom was the worst of it, especially when you were in for a long stretch—and Vinnie was going to be in for a long stretch. Good thing they had a gym—it kept him fit and healthy. He'd be a right bruiser by the time he got out! Now if they only had a pub and a few birds around, he'd be happy as Larry. For a normal red-blooded English bloke like himself not to be able to get his leg over every once in a while, it was no wonder so many ended up doing each other. Not that Vinnie was considering it for a minute. He was as straight as an arrow and always had been. No matter how bad things might get in here, he wasn't batting for the opposition.

As for this business with his brother, he was already greasing the wheels. The great thing about a place like Belmarsh was that a lot of geezers on the inside were well connected with geezers on the outside—the *right* geezers, geezers who could make things happen. And when it did, his toe-rag of a brother wouldn't know what hit him.

Revenge. It had become his new life force, the thing that kept him going. Because *no one* got the better of Vinnie Clark.

Thelonious urged his Mini Cooper past the speed limit, eager to finally be leaving Norfolk behind. He'd had enough of wheat fields and windmills and wide-open skies—they came with too high a price tag. His job here was done, and considering all that had happened, he never wanted to return. Following in the suspected footsteps of the Belgians and Russian, he was heading for the port of Harwich in Essex, where he planned to catch the next ferry to the continent. He didn't care which country it went to as long as it got him out of *this* one.

It had been all over the news about the East End hood who'd been caught, tried and sentenced for the killings of the three publicans in Norfolk. The powers that be wanted to make an example of him, and they'd fast-tracked him through the system, hoping to demonstrate to an increasingly fearful British public that the government was tough on crime. The whole thing had happened so fast it made Thelonious wonder how long the authorities had their man in their sights while he was still being hounded and harassed on the streets of Norfolk by Norfolk CID, only to later become a temporary guest in their jail cell.

The killer's brother was still on the run and wanted as an accessory to murder. Thelonious hoped he'd be found—and soon. To think he'd been happily going about his business when these blood-thirsty killers could have been just a few feet away from him. For all he knew, they might have been casing out one of the pubs he'd gone to, drinking a pint right alongside him. Thelonious tried to remember if he'd seen them at The Drowned Duck, but thankfully could not.

Well, at least it was over with and the police knew who'd done what. Not that this made what had happened to him any less appalling. Thelonious knew he should consider himself lucky that things hadn't been worse. You heard all the time about people being locked up in prison for crimes they didn't commit, left to rot until some self-serving journalist ten or twenty years later decided to make a story out of it. By the time many of these poor buggers got released, they were too old or sick to enjoy their freedom. One of these poor buggers could have been him!

But Thelonious couldn't take any joy from his freedom. On the contrary, he felt cheated. He'd waited around expecting a big apology from local law enforcement, with an appropriate amount of grovelling courtesy of DCI Horatio Sidebottom. Instead he'd been ignored. It wasn't that he wanted anything done in a public way—he'd had enough unwanted attention drawn to himself already. Being arrested on Wickham Marsh high street on a busy weekday morning right across from the letting agent's office where he had an appointment to view a property was definitely at the top of the list for humiliating experiences. It didn't seem right that a decent law-abiding citizen like himself could be treated in this manner. If he'd been a member of any other minority the police would have been bending over backward to smooth the waters lest a riot break out!

The route to Harwich took Thelonious back toward the Broads and he shuddered in the gentle warmth of the afternoon as he passed the turn-off for the boat-hire facility where they'd pulled the body of Augustus Stiffkey from Stanton Broad. He could still hear the abrasive echo of DCI Sidebottom calling out to him from the quay and he pushed the Mini to go faster, as if he could escape the voice inside his head. He soon had to slow down, however, for he was approaching a built-up area. Thelonious hated having to drive at a snail's pace, especially when all he wanted was to get out of here before some other disaster fell on top of his deerstalker hat, but the female voice on the SATNAV kept insisting this was the correct route—a route that would take him straight through the village of Lower Forge and straight past the pub that had been owned by the final victim of what the media collectively referred to as "The Norfolk Killing Spree."

Ye Olde Father. Thelonious saw the pub coming up on his left and he slowed the car to have a better look. In a black attempt at humour, someone had taken paint and altered the sign so that it now read "Ye Olde Farter." A workman wearing white coveralls was in the process of climbing down a tall ladder, having just finished mounting a banner above the entrance.

COMING SOON!
THE WINDMILL INN
A PAOLO LOUIS BLACK PUB

About the Authors

Mitzi Szereto (mitziszereto.com) is an author and anthology editor of multi-genre fiction. She has her own blog, Errant Ramblings: Mitzi Szereto's Weblog and a Web TV channel, Mitzi TV, which covers "quirky" London, England. Her books include *Florida Gothic*; *Oysters and Pearls: Collected Stories*; *The Wilde Passions of Dorian Gray*; *Pride and Prejudice: Hidden Lusts*; *Getting Even: Revenge Stories*; *Dying For It: Tales of Sex and Death*; *Thrones of Desire: Erotic Tales of Swords, Mist and Fire*; *Red Velvet and Absinthe*; *Love, Lust and Zombies* and many other titles. Her anthology *Erotic Travel Tales 2* is the first anthology of erotica to feature a Fellow of the Royal Society of Literature. She divides her time between England and the United States. Find her on Twitter and Facebook.

Teddy Tedaloo (teddytedaloo.com) is co-author of *The Thelonious T. Bear Chronicles* novels. A celebrity teddy bear, trendsetter and world traveller, he's also the publisher and editor of the online newspaper *The Teddy Tedaloo Times* and the production assistant extraordinaire/co-star of Mitzi TV. Popular in social media circles such as Twitter and Facebook, he's known for his entertaining commentary as well as being an animal welfare advocate. He lives (and goes) wherever Mitzi lives (and goes). *Normal for Norfolk (The Thelonious T. Bear Chronicles)* is his first novel in the cosy mystery series featuring ursine protagonist Thelonious T. Bear.

Be sure to watch for more books in *The Thelonious T. Bear Chronicles* series!

Printed in Great Britain
by Amazon